T0090297

The Bouncer

Brian Emburgh

Order this book online at www.trafford.com
or email orders@trafford.com

Most Trafford titles are also available at major online book retailers.

Printed in the United States of America.

ISBN: 978-1-4269-3899-3 (soft)
ISBN: 978-1-4269-3900-6 (ebook)

*Our mission is to efficiently provide the world's finest, most comprehensive
book publishing service, enabling every author to experience success.
To find out how to publish your book, your way, and have it available
worldwide, visit us online at www.trafford.com*

Trafford rev. 8/17/2010

Trafford
PUBLISHING® www.trafford.com

North America & international
toll-free: 1 888 232 4444 (USA & Canada)
phone: 250 383 6864 ♦ fax: 812 355 4082

Dedication

To Brenda and, to old friends who have become
new friends, Gail, Gary and, Johnny

Very Special Acknowledgments

For my Mum and Dad who never
said, "You can't do this, son."

For my daughter Melissa, whose enthusiasm is contagious

Especially to my sister, Diane whose hard
work and tenacity are greatly appreciated

Up and Down and Around We Go

For the most part, John Coyle had a good life. He lived in a spacious mobile home situated on a tree-lined, paved street in a respectable, modern trailer park. The compound boasted a swimming pool, general store, a recreation hall and, a moderately well-equipped gym.

In less than a ten minute drive, when his second-hand Chevrolet wasn't being temperamental, John could purchase such staples as groceries, beer and, oil for the old Cavalier. There was even a well-stocked fry truck located about halfway through the circuit. John knew that he should be avoiding this establishment more than he was inclined.

Although considered somewhat of a loner, John Coyle liked his neighbours and always spoke to them cordially and, in a deferential manner. On several occasions throughout the summer, he would solicit the company of the ancient Mr. Spinelli for the sheer pleasure of sharing some beer or red wine, losing a game of checkers, or simply listening to the old man's remarkable stories. Mr. Spinelli was a short, thin, ramrod erect gentleman with twinkling brown eyes set in a deeply furrowed, malleable face. He had to be eighty but, could remember "the ol' days when I come to this country" with humour and profound alacrity.

John was also fortunate in that by diagonally traversing the highway off of which the park was located, he could arrive at his place of business in less than seven minutes by foot. A moody Chevy was never a factor in marring an excellent attendance record. Mr. Coyle was one of the auspicious people who actually enjoyed his work and was adroit at what he did.

There were excerpts in his life however, that John found disconsolate and unjust. Philosophically, he categorized them as minor annoyances or major compunctions.

On the extreme side of the list, John regretted never having finished university but, the idea of going to work in order to help support an exhausted mother and a younger sister seemed far more important.

He regretted that his father had left when his family needed him most. John had no concept of the whereabouts of his father or if he were even alive. On *most* days, he didn't care. Still, sometimes at night, between wakefulness and sleep…

John Coyle regretted that he had never married and settled in life with the only woman he had ever loved. He had been robbed by an inequitable demigod when his lady had been killed on the highway by a drunk who was too inebrious to recall his act of blind execution.

Perhaps most of all, he regretted the fact, that in all probability, he would never again experience the feeling that only complete, indissoluble commitment to another human being could evoke in a person's heart. That strange combination of yearning, tenderness and, passion might elude him forever. On *some* days, he didn't care.

Primping and Promises

At seven forty-seven p.m., after indulging in a long, cool shower, John Coyle stepped in front of the bathroom mirror to decide if he needed to shave before departing for work. His thick, dark stubble determined that he should.

After completing the task, he retreated to the confines of his small bedroom where the sounds of an old Eagles' tape overcame the steady whir of the air conditioner.

Selecting the traditional black T-shirt from the top drawer of his dresser, and a clean pair of blue jeans from the closet, John dressed slowly. There was still plenty of time before he had to set out. Besides, he wanted to hear the rest of the tape.

What the hell! What's wrong with these pants? John pondered with some bewilderment as he began to thread his belt through the loops. He tried on another pair. And a third. Same result. With considerable effort, he managed to squeeze into the last pair selected. *That's it. No more fry truck for me for a while.* John decided to eject The Eagles' tape and take the circuitous course around the trailer park before crossing the highway to begin his shift. A minor annoyance.

John Coyle was the bouncer at The Sunset Club.

Saturday nights could be quite hectic.

The Delightful Ms. T

At eight forty-three p.m., Mr. Coyle pulled open one of the two heavy steel doors guarding the entrance to the club and proceeded down the dark, cool passageway leading to the main entertainment area. Clean, but, hard to scrub away beer and cigarette smells.

After travelling about fifteen paces, his progress was abruptly halted by a formidable turnstile blocking his passage. John knew what would happen next. He was familiar with the routine.

"Hello, Mr. Barrymore. That wonderful profile of yours is always a sight to behold!"

Turning to his right, toward the source of the voice, John peered through the glass of the small built-in ticket booth and spoke directly into the round, meshed sound hole located about a foot above the ticket slot.

"Good evening, Ms. Taylor and, might I inquire, if I may be so bold, as to the state of your present health?"

Ms. Taylor's real name was Wanda Goldman. Forty years ago, she may have resembled the famed actress in a vague, superficial fashion. Now, with her jet black, obviously dyed bouffant hairdo, painted on brows and heavily rouged puffy cheeks, Mrs. Goldman had evolved into a newspaper caricature of her renowned namesake.

Mrs. Goldman's physical demeanour however, belied an extremely sharp intellect and exceptional verbal creativity. During the eight years that John Coyle had worked at The Sunset, he had never known her to be out a single ticket count or to have missed a single dollar when balancing the club's books. John believed her theatrical salutations were simply an expression to help alleviate the doldrums of a repetitious job. Every night of the work week, people would pay Mrs. Goldman the price of a ticket. She would accept their money, rip the counter in two, pass one half to the customer through the slot and, drop the other piece into a cardboard box situated to the right, on her desk. All cash would be meticulously stowed in a steel receptacle to Mrs. Goldman's left before any other transactions ensued. She would then press a button allowing the stile to rotate and the patron to enter. At the end of the shift, ticket sales and cash received always coincided.

John Coyle and Wanda Goldman took great delight in inventing novel scenarios to perform for each other. Cerebral banter between friends.

Ms. Taylor continued, "Sir, my health is marvellous! Thank you for inquiring. I do look forward however, to the day when this research for my latest cinematographic endeavour will draw to a close. Very tiresome actually."

"Yes, Ms. Taylor, I understand completely. Were it not for…a certain fondness for…distilled products, I too would not be parlaying my talents into such base recompense."

"There are times when we must all bear a weighty cross, sir. Please, enter, gratuitously, of course."

"Thank you, madam. May your research go well this evening."

Ms. Taylor pressed her magic button allowing Mr. Coyle to enter deeper into the realm of illusion.

Inside the Shadowbox

The main room, or entertainment centre of The Sunset Club, comprised the first floor of the two story cinder block structure. The Playroom.

A large hardwood stage dominated the hub of the spacious chamber, complete with an overhanging mirrored globe and, traditional brass pole. Track lighting, focusing on the stage, could be set to flash automatically in sync with the music.

A narrow, carpeted runway originated from an ornate doorway to the stage. Stairs descending from the second floor dressing room led to a small waiting platform behind the elaborate portal.

Along the east side of the room, parallel to the runway and, taking up more than half of the length of the expanse, ran the polished mahogany bar. Ceiling to floor wall-mounted mirrors reflected the myriad of bottles situated behind the bar. The mirrors gave the entire hall a distorted sense of endless dimension.

A modest kitchen set behind the same wall from which the bar protruded provided simple, but ample fare for the hungry. The window from which harried waitresses could place and receive orders was always busy. A saloon-style swinging door connected the kitchen to the entertainment centre.

Along the west wall, a dozen old diner inspired booths provided a certain degree of privacy and comfort for those inclined to indulge.

Scattered strategically throughout the remaining floor space were numerous, small tables and comfortable chairs from which customers could eat, drink, watch the show or simply talk.

Three clearly marked exits, two located on the north wall on either side of the runway and, one on the west wall splitting the row of booths, led to the expansive asphalt parking lot which framed The Sunset.

Two washrooms labelled "Gentlemen" and, "Ladies" and, divided by a common cinder block wall, were situated to the left of the entrance on the south wall. Each was neat and exceptionally clean.

This comprised the shadowbox.

This was John Coyle's turf.

Denizens of the Deep

The first thing that the bouncer noticed upon stepping into his precinct, was the reverberating, thumping notes of a bass guitar pounding out the rhythm of an extremely monotonous song through the club's sound system. *Please, God, cause the sub-woofer to explode*, he entreated in his mind. A minor annoyance if there ever were one.

Passing in front of the kitchen area, on his way to the bar, John paused briefly to exchange greetings with Molly, whose pretty face was framed by the open window of her domain. Bending his six feet frame slightly, so as to be on the same level as the cook, John spoke first: "Hi, Molly. How are you? Pretty quiet for a Saturday night."

"Yes, so far, John but, I imagine things should start to get busy soon enough."

"You're right about that, Molly. See you later."

"See you later, John."

Molly had been working at the club for about a year but, apart from their nightly regards, the bouncer had never really come to know her. She wore her dirty blonde hair buried under a white corrugated cardboard chef's hat and, whenever John had seen her leave the kitchen, her tall figure had been concealed by loose fitting white slacks and a matching blouse. A crisp apron was always draped over the ensemble. John Coyle had also noticed that the young lady had very large, very blue eyes.

Such was not the case with The Sunset's proprietor. After taking leave of Molly, John sauntered the few paces to the bar where he was greeted by Mr. Charlie Kmetzko, owner and chief bartender of the club. The gentleman was short, thin, balding and, very pallid of complexion. His beady blue eyes always seemed to be watering. John thought that Charlie might be allergic to his station in life.

"Evening, John."

"Good evening, Charlie. How are you tonight?" John knew the answer before it was delivered.

"I feel like crap, John. I haven't slept real good in about twenty years and my back is killin' me. Can't wait to retire and get out of this freakin' business."

"Well, boss, it wouldn't be the same around here without you."

"Thanks, my friend but, sometimes I feel real old." Charlie might have been fifty. Thirteen years older than John.

"Well, I see that Delbert is starting to set up. See if I can talk him into playing some real music in between shows." John wanted to change the subject. Sometimes his employer's negativity could become tedious. "Later, boss."

"God willing, I'll be here, John."

Delbert Kmetzko noticed John's approach from the opposite end of the bar and rose from his table behind the polished mahogany slab to greet the bouncer. Delbert was the sound and light man and, announcer at the club. He was responsible for playing the songs that the dancers had selected for their routines as well as providing background music between shows. The young Mr. Kmetzko also introduced the various acts and announced nightly food specials emanating from the kitchen. Although the nephew of Mr. Charlie Kmetzko, John was positive that there was no nepotism involved in Delbert's placement. Even though Kmetzko, Junior performed quite an admirable job at The Sunset, Kmetzko, Senior belittled his young liege at every given opportunity. Still, Delbert refused to bend which was quite a remarkable feat for the towering, emaciated looking spinner of tunes. Senior's verbal barrages, delivered at close quarters had the power to fell mighty oaks. "So, Delbert, what's happening?" inquired John, with a smile, as the two shook hands.

"Nothing much, my man. Just putting the songs in order and hopin' the cats will dig what the Delster has to offer. Hopin' everything is a groove." Junior stroked his sparse goatee and shrugged his boney shoulders.

Why does this kid talk like this? pondered John.

Hoping to reassure Delbert, the bouncer replied with exaggerated sincerity: "Everything will be cool, Del. Nobody's better than you."

"Thanks, man. Appreciate your positive vibes!" Delbert smiled.

"Oh, by the way, Del, have you ever considered playing something a little different between acts? Maybe something, let's say, by The Eagles?" John pressed on. "Could be a blast, man!"

Delbert appeared thoughtful. "Okay, big guy. If you get me some of the music, I'll give it a listen to. Could be pretty decent."

"Okay, Del. It's a deal. I'll bring you some Monday night."

The two men once again shook hands. This time, it was to solidify their agreement.

John Coyle departed in order to commence work.

The room was beginning to fill.

Saturday nights could be quite hectic.

All in a Night's Work

At precisely nine thirty p.m., Delbert Kmetzko announced the opening act of the evening's agenda. "Ladies and gentlemen, welcome to The Sunset! Tonight, for your enjoyment, directly from Hollywood, California, U.S.A., we are proud to present Miss Linda McLuscious!"

Following that grandiose proclamation, the door leading to the carpeted path flew open, flashing spotlights illuminated the runway, a thumping melody by B.B. Joey G. pumped through massive speakers and, Miss McLuscious took her first high heeled step onto the road to fame and fortune.

The club opener, upon reaching the stage, waited for the correct musical cue and, began her performance. Wrapping her lithe body around the brass pole, she twisted and gyrated to the racing pulse of the hedonistic beat. Her ebony hair flew to the rhythm of the music. Her hips thrust and recoiled in perfect tempo. She was poetry on a pole.

At the end of her act, her many supporters expressed their profound approval with catcalls and whistles of approbation. Linda McLuscious was a hit!

John Coyle smiled to himself.

Not all of the performers would be so well received. It was club policy that a very pretty, very enthusiastic dancer would open the show. At the end of the twenty minute routine, there would be a comparable recess which gave customers time to drink and reflect upon the opening act. Another performer would then take possession of the stage. Some were good, others, not so talented. The headliner usually appeared around eleven thirty. Customers normally stayed to view the remaining acts, wondering if a dancer could possibly surpass the eleven thirty performer. By one ten, when the last dancer had finished her act, clients could order another drink, down it, and vacate the room by two. Clever conditioning on the part of Mr. Charlie Kmetzko, acquired through years of experience.

Tonight, along with the lovely Miss McLuscious, The Sunset Club also boasted such rare talents as Nancy Neutron, Dee Dee Delight and, Miss Olga Oglesworthy. Lotta Cleavage had the privilege of headlining the show.

The second floor of The Sunset was divided into six small, but neat and clean apartments. A comfortable dressing room was also located on the second floor. A narrow hallway fronting the living areas and dressing room was bisected by stairs leading down to the entertainment centre. Three apartments on one side of the stairway, three apartments, plus the dressing room, on the other. The dressing room was directly adjacent to the east side of the staircase for the dancers' convenience.

Rates were very reasonable but, if the dancers chose different lodgings, the prerogative was theirs.

Acts were usually booked for a week's duration but, policy was flexible. There were always exceptions.

For John Coyle, the evening passed quickly and relatively uneventfully. He knew the routine and what to expect. Years on the job had transformed him into a keen observer of human behaviour and a stickler for details. John also had a basic aversion to pain. He much preferred a quiet discussion over displays of machismo. Although Charlie could press a button on the bar phone and summon the police in moments, a reassuring nod from the bouncer often prevented this procedure from being hastily employed. John was a strong proponent of the spoken word and relied upon physicality only as a last resort.

Tonight, The Sunset's warden had to summon a taxi for two drunks after persuading them that driving home would not be prudent. Their car could be locked and left in the parking lot. Pick it up tomorrow. No trouble.

At around ten, someone departed the club through one of the exits. A few moments later, having had a change of intent, the gentleman tried to re-enter by pounding on the steel door in hopes that someone would let him in. John opened the door for him and politely explained that exits were meant for only one purpose. The bouncer allowed the customer access however, "just this one time." The errant patron thanked John profusely and quietly made his way to the bar. No problem.

Subduing a very obnoxious, very vociferous heckler took a little more imagination. Gently guiding the loudmouth to a quiet corner, John, in a restrained, conspiratorial voice, unleashed his magic in the hall of mirrors: "Sir, and I call you that out of respect because I feel you are a real gentleman, I agree with you one-hundred percent. The lady is not very good at all. You are a keen judge of talent, my friend."

The heckler nodded and smiled. He was beginning to like the bouncer.

John Coyle continued: "I have to tell you something though, sir. About three months ago, the lady's husband left her for a pink-haired singer in a punk band. He also left the lady with a year-old baby girl to support. The lady's trying everything she can to make a few dollars. I can tell you have a good heart and, like myself, would somehow like to help. Any ideas, sir?"

"Well," he began…"I…see what you mean. Yep. You're right! It's not fair! When she's finished, I'm gonna slip her a five. No! A ten! Maybe some of the other guys will do the same."

"Sir," John responded in a sombre tone, "I was right. You are a gentleman. It's been a real pleasure meeting you."

The bouncer offered his hand. The two men shook.

John resumed his rounds.

At the end of her performance, the dancer was mystified by the unexpected generosity of her former critic.

Minor annoyances in a night's work. That's all.

Even Bouncers Rest
on the Sabbath

Sunday was John's day of rest.

Except for a crew of cleaning staff, the club was closed.

Rising about noon, Mr. Coyle made himself a ham, onion and, red pepper omelette, with brown toast and a pot of steaming coffee. He ate slowly and meticulously cleared the table and washed his dishes.

Fifty minutes later, he began his workout at the park's gym. John could still accomplish the same gruelling weight routines he handled at twenty-five. It just took a bit longer.

An hour later, the exhausted warrior showered, changed his clothes, and, trudged the short distance back to his trailer.

Once inside his home, he emptied his worn gym bag of its odoriferous contents and stowed the antiquated piece of luggage in the bedroom closet. Next, John withdrew a sturdy plastic bag from a kitchen drawer, removed four frosty bottles of Corona from the refrigerator and, gently packed the treasures into the sack. *Maybe, with these offerings, Mr. Spinelli might let me win a game,* John thought. *Maybe not.* The hopeful sportsman packed an extra two bottles.

When John Coyle arrived at his friend's trailer a few moments later, he was pleased to see that the elderly gentleman was already seated beneath a large green, white and, red umbrella situated on his deck. The checkers game was set up. Mr. Spinelli was drinking red wine. He noticed John's approach.

"Hello, John! Come on up. Wanna play a few games with this tired old man?"

"Sure, thanks, Mr. Spinelli but, if you're so old and tired, how come I never win?"

Mr. Spinelli laughed. "I think, my younga friend, is because you see, you understand good an' you…react very responsively. You can be tricked though. You no perfect. You no Superman."

Mr. Coyle smiled and nodded. "Maybe you're right, Mr. Spinelli. I've always been a sucker for a pretty face."

"You crazy!" Mr. Spinelli laughed. "You really think I'm pretty?"

The six-pack, a half bottle of wine and, five games of checkers passed quickly. Mr. Spinelli won all five games.

"Mr. Spinelli, I don't think I'm ever gonna beat you. You're just too good."

"John, my boy, sure you can. You jus' needa some… persistence. Tella you what. I go an' get another bottle. You sit an' think about…my…motives. Okay?"

"Okay." John thought. Nothing seemed to be registering.

When most of the new bottle had been consumed, John felt his luck begin to turn. He had won the last two moves!

A concerned Mr. Spinelli confirmed Mr. Coyle's bright prospects. "John, maybe this is the game. If you beat me, I will come to your house next Sunday, with great humility. We can play again if you like. I mucha enjoyed the beer today. Perhaps, you could buy more. Red wine, not too sweet, also makes competition most pleasant. Pizza is good with beer an' wine. What you think, John? Do we have the deal?"

"We sure do, Mr. Spinelli! And, thanks!"

John Coyle won his first game of checkers with Mr. Spinelli just as the last bottle of wine was drained. He was jubilant! He had dethroned the master!

Slowly, the triumphant strategist rose to his feet and extended his hand to the fallen old lion. "Thanks again, Mr. Spinelli. Please come by a bit early next Sunday so that we can have some lunch before we play."

"Thank you, John. I will be most delighted." Mr. Spinelli smiled impishly.

John departed for home.

As he turned the key to unlock his trailer, the new champ of the checkers board stopped abruptly at the sound of the click. *Wait a minute! He beat me again! I didn't see the move coming and I'm supposed to be good at stuff like that. Never too old to learn.*

John Coyle grinned. *Yeah, maybe Mr. Spinelli is right. I'm no Superman.*

Mystic Monday

Arriving at The Sunset Club shortly before nine on Monday night, afforded John plenty of time to cajole with the lovely Ms. Taylor, patiently listen to Charlie complain about the inequities of his existence and, deliver a satchel of tapes and CD's to Mr. Delbert Kmetzko.

As per custom and necessity, Ms. Taylor was the bouncer's first encounter.

"Good evening, Mr. Barrymore. Prepared to fend off the legion of lady admirers? Take my advice, sir. Be diligent lest you are silhouetted by a roving spotlight. That, sir, could mean trouble."

"Ms. Taylor, I certainly value your sage words and will heed your wise counsel tonight. Tell me though, dear lady, how is your research progressing?"

"Sir, to be honest, there are days when I don't fully understand my director's vision in this matter. Still, I bow to his perspicacity."

"And that is why you are one of the greatest actresses of all time, Ms. Taylor!"

"Thank you, Mr. Barrymore. Please enter."

John passed through the enchanted portal and entered into his arena of expertise.

Charlie, the proprietor extraordinaire, was slumped across the bar and in the process of blowing his nose when the bouncer joined him.

"Hey, Charlie, is everything okay? You look a little down tonight." John did his best to add just the right touch of sympathy to his voice.

"Oh, I can't believe it. Nothin' worse than a summer cold, my friend. I can hardly breathe and, look at my eyes! Looks like I'm freakin' cryin'!"

John looked but, saw nothing out of the ordinary.

"Yeah, I see what you mean, boss. Maybe you should have stayed home and called somebody in."

"I wouldn't wish this freakin' job on my worst enemy, John, but if it gets any worse, I may as well just put a bullet through my head!"

Several tears fell upon the bar as if to accentuate Charlie's last assertion.

John was positive they were the product of his employer's malady but, tried to appear respectfully concerned.

"Okay, Charlie but, try to take it easy tonight."

As the bouncer took his leave, he decided to knock on the kitchen door and order a juicy burger and gravy-laden plate of fries from Molly before his shift officially began. The salad he had prepared and picked at for dinner just didn't satiate his hunger. John's willpower soon overrode his desire for high caloric nourishment however. *Nope*, he thought, *I refuse to buy bigger jeans.*

Instead, the hungry young man reversed his direction, giving Charlie a wide berth, and, in a few steps, found himself facing Delbert Kmetzko and his impressive array of audio accoutrements.

"Hey, Del! What's happening?" John simply raised his hand in greeting. He couldn't remember what the hip handshake of the week was.

"Yo, John! Not much, my man. Is that the music you said you'd deliver for my listening pleasure?"

"Sure is, Del. I know you'll think some of it is pretty cool, if you just give it a chance."

"Will do, amigo. I'll give 'em a spin tomorrow. Thanks for layin' the melodies on me."

John surrendered the tunes to the music man.

The jockey continued: "Wow, man! Speaking of music, I was just going over each dancer's music one more time before the show and, some of this stuff is pretty trippy, man. Should be a far-out week."

"Who's on stage this week, Del? Any new faces?" asked John. Even after years on the job, he always found Monday nights exciting. New performers. Diverse routines. Novel music. Showtime!

"Oh yeah, my friend! I think there may be some groovy new ladies tonight, man. Dig some of the names, if you will!" Without skipping a beat, the club's announcer delivered a condensed preview of the evening's events. "Tonight, with profound delectation, The Sunset Club is proud to present Miss Symantha Romanca, Fanny Fanny and, Bricka House! Headlining our spectacular extravaganza is the one and only, Driven Miss Daisy!"

Both men laughed. Not at the performers themselves. Never at the performers. Just at the inventive way each had of defining her original identity.

"Okay, sounds good, Delbert. Better get to work. Talk to you later."

Delbert nodded, made the appropriate gesture and uttered, "Peace."

John smiled and abandoned his young friend. The bouncer needed to assume his first vantage point of the night. The exit located on the west wall seemed as good a place as any to commence his vigil. By selecting this location, Mr. Coyle could also procure a panoramic view of the opening act. One learned a few tricks after so many years.

Monday nights were always unpredictable at The Sunset Club. New acts drew in the curious but, John always felt there was something deeper than the "moths drawn to a fire" metaphor. It almost seemed to him that the vast majority of the club's guests were there to energize themselves with enough illusory sensualism to sustain them through four more days of jobs they detested. John understood their plight. There were times he had fallen into the same rut. No more.

Tonight found the crowd extremely well-behaved. There were two under aged kids who had to be shown the door but, by employing a bit of Irish charm, no trouble ensued as a result. By refunding their ticket money and promising to buy them a beer in another year, the bouncer practically assured The Sunset of two steady customers in the near future.

At precisely ten twenty, Long Tall Sally, the club's second act hit the stage quite literally. With her show halfway finished, the six feet three Amazon attempted an unwieldy pirouette, stumbled, broke the heel of her left shoe, fell to the floor of the stage, twisted her well-turned ankle and, sat there sobbing in pain and profound humiliation.

The crowd grew silent. John Coyle looked at Charlie Kmetzko for direction. Charlie Kmetzko shrugged and poured himself a drink. Molly emerged through the kitchen door and gazed at John beseechingly. He had to do something. Maintaining the status quo was his responsibility.

Reacting on instinct and propriety, John Coyle leapt upon the stage, placed Sally's left arm over his sturdy right shoulder, hoisted the dancer so she was leaning upon him and, acting as a human crutch, began to assist the young lady back down the runway to the dressing room.

The hushed assemblage erupted in cheers and whistles! John wasn't sure for whom the applause was intended.

A few moments later, after making sure that Sally was resting comfortably and that medical attention was forthcoming, the bouncer emerged through the runway door. Again, the crowd expressed itself in vociferous, prolonged approbation. John blushed. He glanced at Molly who was still standing outside her corner of the club. She returned his look with one of admiration. John turned a deeper shade of red.

The rest of the evening paled in comparison.

Mondays. Who knows?

Whistling While at Work

For the befriender of dancers in distress, the remainder of the work week passed quickly with several positive highlights appearing throughout.

On Tuesday night, John was pleasantly surprised to be greeted by the tight harmonies of The Eagles singing "Hotel California" as he stepped into the club's inner sanctum. He had to admit that the tune sounded infinitely superior when played over expensive equipment than it did when going through his simple combination radio and tape/CD player. Thanking Delbert and complimenting him on his selection of material, John was quickly reminded of his friend's musical prowess when the disc jockey innocently stated: "This is a mind-blowing song, my man but, I wonder what an acoustic version would sound like."

The following evening, a fatalistic Mr. Coyle reluctantly decided to confront his employer in order to ascertain the degree to which the dreaded cold had incapacitated Charlie.

I know what's coming, thought John *but, after all, he does sign my cheques.*

Mr. Kmetzko's response was astounding; diametrically opposed to his entire character. "I feel great, John! Got some over-the-counter pills from the drugstore and feel like a million freakin' bucks! Life is good, my boy!"

John mused. *Yeah, and life can be strange.*

On Thursday evening, while stationed near the exit to the right of the runway, John noticed a wallet lying on the floor about two feet from where he stood. Picking it up, he realized his find was quite plump. Very weighty. Bulging.

A few moments later, after John had asked Delbert to announce the discovery of the lost billfold, the security man was confronted by a gentleman who bore a striking similarity to the recovered acquisition. Quite plump. Very weighty. Bulging. John felt instinctively that he must be the owner. After checking the picture identification in one of the plastic card protectors, a positive match was affirmed.

The portly gentleman was expeditious in expressing his gratitude. "Sir, my name is Mike Murphy, owner of 'Murphy's Meats'. I'd sure like to reward your honesty." Sausage-like fingers began to probe his fat wallet.

"No, sir, that's not necessary. I was just doing my job. I can't accept any reward, although it was generous of you to offer." John Coyle was not the kind of man to take advantage of a situation.

Mr. Murphy pressed on. "I understand but, at least let me give you these." Doughy digits changed direction and withdrew several loose coupons from the portly meat monger's shirt pocket. "These are gift certificates, my friend for packages of one-hundred percent all beef wieners. They're the best we make! The certificates are redeemable at any of our two convenient locations. Please take them as a token of my appreciation."

"Well," replied John, "I guess this would be okay. Thank you very much."

It was a stout gesture.

At about eleven, the next night, part of a minor motorcycle gang rode into Dodge with the sole intent of proving that they were the town's new top guns. There were five of them: all big, all greasy, all dressed in their club's colours, all foul-mouthed, all intent on demonstrating individual beer capacity and, all bound and determined to initiate a fight.

John Coyle had seen their kind before. Individually, each was likely to back down when confronted one-on-one. In a pack however, a collective mentality emerged. Each member could be dangerous. The watchman wanted no trouble from The Lonesome Desperados.

After nearly half an hour of listening to abusive language and witnessing harassing behaviour aimed toward waitresses, dancers, and nearby customers, John had had enough. Twice, he had respectfully requested that the gang members watch their language and not bother other people. Twice, he was ignored. John looked to Charlie. Charlie nodded. Time to act.

Exiting through the front entrance, after bestowing a solemn, conspiratorial gesture of understanding upon Ms. Taylor, John found himself in the front parking lot where he immediately found what he knew he would encounter: five beautifully painted, highly chromed, radically customized, and, very expensive motorcycles parked in a neat, straight row near the front entrance.

Without a moment's hesitation, he made his way to what he considered the most stunning of the machines, paused, and spat upon the highly lacquered gas tank.

John Coyle turned, retraced his steps, entered through one of the double doors, smiled and nodded to Ms. Taylor, passed through the deactivated stile and, dashed with conviction to the bikers' table.

Addressing the biggest and roughest looking lout, John hurriedly began his tale of woe. "Look, man, I know those must be your rides outside. Righteous. About a minute ago, I went outside to have a little 'smoke' break, if you know what I mean. Three assholes ran away from your scoots, jumped in a blue Toyota pickup parked in the handicapped zone and took off. They shot me the finger and laughed as they laid rubber! I checked your bikes, man, and saw they spit on the red one with the flames. A Toyota, man,! They can't be more than a couple of miles away. I ran right in to tell you. Little punks!"

Big Bear growled. "Okay, which way they head?"

"West, man!"

"Mount up, men! And…thanks, bud. We owe you."

With that pledge of gratitude, John escorted his newfound friends through the front entrance and, to their bikes.

When the leader noticed the smear on his tank, he immediately wiped it away with the filthy bandanna stowed in his back pocket. He then returned the overblown handkerchief to his pocket while growling even louder.

Once the quintet had roared away into the night, John imagined himself blowing the smoke away from the barrel of his Colt .45 and holstering the weapon with a twirl and a slap of leather.

His town was safe for another day.

Saturday Night and Cinderella Leaves the Ball

As usual, the kitchen closed at midnight on Saturdays and, as usual, Molly abandoned her kingdom of the griddle shortly after.

What was different tonight however, was the fact that she had forsaken her culinary garb for apparel far more alluring, at least in the humble opinion of Mr. John Coyle.

Molly's black denim miniskirt accentuated long, shapely legs and, a white sleeveless cotton top highlighted her ample feminine assets.

The cook was tall but, certainly not skinny.

Molly noticed John noticing her. She smiled and began walking toward him. As she approached, the doorman beheld long, dark lashes framing expressive gray-blue eyes and full, almost pouting lips, complimenting even white teeth. Molly's short blonde hair appeared very soft.

"Well, that's it for me, John. Have a good day tomorrow. See you Monday."

"Okay, Molly. You too." The bouncer could think of nothing clever to say. "Oh, by the way, you look really nice tonight. Special occasion?"

"Nope." Molly smiled. "Just felt like getting out of my dress whites a bit early."

Again, John's rejoinder was not as inspired as hoped. "Well, 'bye then, Molly."

"'Bye, John."

Molly turned and set out for life outside The Sunset.

John murmured something to himself. It probably wasn't that profound.

Checkered Pasts

John awoke earlier on Sunday morning than was his wont and prerogative. Throughout the night, he had dreamed sporadically of a blonde, blue-eyed Lois Lane with whom he had shared numerous, though often disjointed adventures. The episodes were recurrently most pleasant.

On one such occasion, a somewhat self-conscious Mr. Coyle, attired in blue tights which were far too constrictive around his waist, had rescued Miss Lane from a huge Kodiak bear riding a Harley-Davidson. The furry beast had attempted to capture Lois in the demented hope of forcing the young damsel into a life of servitude within the cave walls of his murky den. Here, the fair maiden would be compelled, by sordid means, to prepare endless platters of succulent hamburgers to appease the ravenous monster's carnal appetite!

The Man-in-the-Blue-Tights would never allow this morbid scenario to unfold. By dropping a huge checker piece from the roof of a two story cinder block building, he was able to knock the villain from the seat of his speeding motorcycle and swoop the heroine into his arms before she fell from her tiny leather perch on the bike's rear fender.

Afterward, the enamoured couple had somehow found its way to John's Fortress of Seclusion. The Fortress bore a striking resemblance to a conventional trailer. Once nestled safely within its protective, yet thin walls, Mr. Coyle and Miss Lane had quaffed sugar-free beer and munched on watercress and Melba toast.

Weird dream, thought John as he shrugged off a momentary notion of symbolic analysis. *Nice bike though.*

Time for energy ingestion. Vital to caloric expenditure. Four egg whites whipped into an omelette, one piece of dry multigrain toast and, a tall glass of papaya juice would provide all the fuel required for a decent workout.

On the way to the park's gym, John planned his session.

On the way back to his home, John planned his recuperation.

The workout, lasting a little more than an hour, had been more gruelling than John had first envisioned. Perhaps, the previous night's disjointed sleep pattern had been a contributing factor. Perhaps, a more substantial source of nutrients was required.

After twenty sets of bicep and tricep exercises, the bouncer's upper arms felt like they were about to explode. A combination of free weights and machine movements had accomplished the desired effect. Progress hurts. At least the self-inflicted anguish was finished for the day.

After showering, John was pleasantly surprised to discover that the first pair of clean jeans selected from his closet fit snuggly but, not inordinately tightly. Two more fittings, two more similar results. *Man*, he pondered, *I hope*

I'm not becoming anorexic. That would not be too condusive to my chosen profession. The bouncer smiled.

Since Mr. Spinelli had promised to come a bit early for lunch, Mr. Coyle set about making sure that all was arranged prior to his friend's arrival. The pizza was ready to pop into the oven, a tray of freshly prepared assorted vegetables had been meticulously placed around a vessel of low-cal dip and, beer and medium-sweet wine were chilling in the fridge. John's kitchen table had been cleared and his checkers set was ready to see combat.

At shortly after twelve, John Coyle responded to a knock on his door. It was Mr. Spinelli.

"Hi, Mr. Spinelli."

Mr. Spinelli smiled and raised a wrinkled hand in greeting. "Hello, my friend."

Through the open door, John motioned to one of a set of comfortable canvas lawn chairs placed around a white plastic table on his deck. "Have a seat and I'll be right with you. I'm just gonna pop the pizza into the oven and get us something to drink. What would you like to start off with?"

"I wouldn't mind a little red wine, if you have some, John."

"Coming right up! I bought four bottles of your favourite when it was on sale the other day."

John closed the trailer door. A moment later, he reappeared with a translucent green bottle and two glasses. Placing the wine and glasses on the table, John seated himself across the table from his elderly checkers companion and filled the glasses with chilled vermilion libation.

Passing a glass to his octogenarian gaming partner, John raised his goblet to salute his venerable crony.

"Here's to you, Mr. Spinelli, and, the beautiful day."

Mr. Spinelli reciprocated. "An' to you, John an' your generosity!"

The two drank deeply.

John poured another round.

"The pizza should be ready, Mr. Spinelli. I can bring it out if you'd like to eat out here."

"Please, no bother, John. Is such a lazy afternoon that we can eat anytime. Let's jus' have a little wine and enjoy the sunshine."

"Sounds like the perfect plan, Mr. Spinelli. I can bring the checkers set out later too. Whenever we feel like a game or two. Care for a bit more wine?"

"That would be an excellent idea, my friend. An excellent idea!"

Within thirty minutes, the first bottle of wine had been drained.

"Care for something to eat now, Mr. Spinelli or would you like some more wine? I've got lots in the fridge. Beer too."

"I wouldn't mind a little more wine, if is no trouble, younga man. Today reminds me of Sundays a long time ago. Sun. Wine. Good friends." Mr. Spinelli seemed to momentarily drift off to a private place.

Mr. Coyle drifted off to fetch another bottle.

When he returned, the two friends resumed the indolent indulgence.

A glass was enjoyed in comfortable silence.

It was John who broke the spell.

"Mr. Spinelli, if you don't mind my asking, what was it like in your old country? You've spoken about the early days here but, never about your life before your arrival. You can tell me to mind my own business, my friend and, I promise I won't be offended."

"No is okay, John. Is jus' I remember mucha but, no talk too mucha."

Mr. Spinelli's accent seemed to be growing stronger in direct proportion to his alcohol consumption.

John interpreted his friend's assertion as a sublime signal to satisfy his curiosity.

"What did you do back in the old country, Mr. Spinelli?" It seemed to John that the question was not too intrusive. A good springboard for exploring unknown depths.

"I worka inna the bank of my town."

"Sounds impressive. Did you enjoy the banking business, Mr. Spinelli?"

Mr. Spinelli's thin lips twisted into a satanic grimace and his complexion visibly reddened. "I hate every minute of job! I hate bosses! I hate work of paper! I hate every son-of-a-fungus-covered-grape I worka with! What coulda I do? I needed money. Had…the responsibilities."

John was immediately sorry that he had broached the subject of his friend's past means of employment. He was however, very impressed with Mr. Spinelli's grape imagery.

John pressed on. "Was a family part of those responsibilities, Mr. Spinelli?" Perhaps subject matter of a more benevolent nature might help to lower Mr. Spinelli's blood pressure.

"Si, I hadda most beautiful an' lovely woman inna village as wife." The lines in Mr. Spinelli's face seemed to soften and a whimsical smile replaced the snarl on his mouth.

John was pleased with his second choice of inquiries.

"What happened to her, Mr. Spinelli?"

"She die. One day, circus come to village. We buy tickets, go to big top. 'Tony, The Human Cannonball' be main attraction. Beautiful costume he wear. Silver cape. Silver helmet. He go inna big gun. Big gunfire. Boom! Tony fly through air like baby jet plane with a blue smoke chasing it. Too mucha of explosive. Tony fly too far. He crash. He crash into beautiful an' lovely wife! He kill her."

A single tear rolled over the furrows of Mr. Spinelli's weathered cheek and his bottom lip began to quiver sporadically.

John Coyle was devastated. How could he have infringed upon his friend's privacy to such a horrific extent? Shame and guilt intermingled with a strong appreciation of Mr. Spinelli's colourful jet simile.

Perhaps a bit more wine would help to assuage Mr. Spinelli's frazzled emotions. John poured. The two drank.

Mr. Spinelli spoke first. "You wanna know what happen to 'Tony, The Human Cannonball', killer of beautiful an' lovely wife, John?"

"Sure I do but, I just didn't want to upset you by asking, old friend. Have another glass and tell me if you are so inclined."

More wine was disposed of.

"'Tony, The Human Cannonball' be badly bruise after he kill beautiful an' lovely wife. He even broka his leg. He live though. Shortly after, Mr. Cannonball meet with most terrible and…permanent accident. He was found inna his bed inna circus trailer with roll of coins stuffed down throat. Bad way to die. Strange, but I hear that name of my bank was printed on roll of coins."

A smile appeared on Mr. Spinelli's face and, for just a moment, he appeared several years younger.

"Immediately following tragic event, I come to this country."

Mr. Spinelli chuckled.

Mr. Coyle left the table to retrieve another bottle.

Within a moment, he was once again seated opposite his garrulous guest.

He's gotta be kidding about the whole story, John surmised as he cracked the seal on the third bottle. *What an imagination though. He really had me going for a while.*

"Would you like some lunch now, Mr. Spinelli?" John strived to be a good host.

"No, thank you, John. I have mucha good time jus' drinking an' engaging in…social discourse!" Mr. Spinelli valiantly attempted to regain mastery of his second language. His eloquence would not be diminished by base spirits.

"That's okay. That's fine. Your command is my wish, partner!" *Maybe I'd better slow down a bit*, thought John. *Next thing ya know, I'll have an Italian accent.*

Messrs. Coyle and Spinelli toasted each other's health.

The elder of the two gentlemen, in hopes of reciprocity, posed an inquiry of his own. "I know you no worka for nightclub forever, John. What you do before? Is okay I ask?"

"Sure, it's okay, Mr. Spinelli."

John took a drink.

"I've done a lot of things. I worked up north in the mines. Put in time as a security guard for about a year. Even helped run a music store for a while. Believe it or not, I also attended university for two years."

"Why you no finish, John?"

"Oh, you know. Same stuff that happens to everybody. Struggling mother. Little sister. No father around. There were bills. Rent to pay. Turned out okay though. My mum passed away several years ago. She was fat and happy. A real lady. My sister married and is doing really well. I usually see her at Christmas. She and her husband are expecting their third child. Nice family."

"Why you not go back to school now, John? Never too old, as they say."

John Coyle hesitated. He wasn't sure if he wanted to continue or if he were even capable. He took a breath and a drink.

"The time I spent at school was the happiest I've ever been. I was engaged to a wonderful, caring young woman who loved me as much as I loved her. Her name was Sarah.

We lived in a small, barely furnished apartment but, to us, it was a mansion. Sarah worked full-time as a receptionist for a small law firm. After school, I cleaned equipment and put weights away at a gym.

"My mum wasn't doing too badly then but, she and my sister still needed my help to manage.

"Most days, I stayed at school and studied until about five. Sarah would pick me up in her second-hand Volkswagon and we'd laugh and talk about our day until we got back to our place. We'd have a light supper and I'd be off to the gym for a couple of hours. Sarah would pick me up after work and we'd drive home. It gave us more time to laugh and talk. It seemed we were always laughing. We'd…"

John had to stop. His eyes had become bleary and his throat constricted.

"You okay, John? You no hafta finish story, my friend." Mr. Spinelli spoke softly and emitted unabashed empathy.

"I'm okay, thanks, Mr. Spinelli. I just needed a minute."

John Coyle continued. "One day, Sarah didn't show up at the gym to pick me up. I figured that maybe she was catching up with paper work at the office and didn't have time to phone. My boss at the gym was a good guy and let me put in a little extra overtime of my own. About an hour later, I received a visitor. It was a police officer. Sarah was dead. She was killed by a drunk on her way to pick me up."

"God, I so sorry, my friend." Mr. Spinelli's voice quaked and his eyes misted over.

"What can you do, Mr. Spinelli? From then on, nothing mattered as much as it once did. A major compunction, Mr. Spinelli. A major compunction."

For the next half hour, both men sat in silence. They sipped wine and reflected upon life's dividends and iniquities.

When the third bottle of wine had been emptied, Mr. Spinelli turned to his younger friend and smiled.

"You know, John, this was excellent afternoon. We tella stories, drink wine an' sit inna sun. Life is good!"

"You're right, Mr. Spinelli. This has been a good afternoon. Life is good and you're a good friend." John reached across the table, grinned and shook his confidant's hand.

Slowly, Mr. Spinelli rose from his chair. "These old bones sometimes become…wearisome. I go now an' perhaps take the small nap. Thank you for the most wonderful afternoon of…candid interaction."

"Thank you, Mr. Spinelli. Maybe next time, we'll actually play checkers!"

Both laughed.

Mr. Spinelli languidly made his way homeward.

For the rest of the afternoon and, into mid-evening, John Coyle sat on his deck and enjoyed the solitude and his memories.

Just Prior to One of Those Strange Moments in Life

"Ahh, Ms. Taylor, the start of another week of relentless travail for those of us not born with the proverbial silver spoon!"

"Yes, Mr. Barrymore, a profound and very astute observation of the human condition. By the way, sir, have you received any encouraging news from your agent concerning forthcoming cinematic projects?"

"Alas, fair lady, I have nothing *concrete* to report. I have *heard* however, that several studios *may* be interested in my services provided details can be ironed out to the mutual satisfaction of all parties involved. I have ascertained, through the grapevine, the film involves the dramatic exploits of a young pugilist on the road to attaining success in his chosen field of endeavour."

"What!" exclaimed Ms. Taylor. "I strongly urge you as a friend, sir to seriously think about accepting such a role!

Please remember your trademark attribute. Were anything of a damaging nature to occur to your renowned silhouette, forthcoming portrayals as the greatest of all lovers may be greatly diminished."

"As usual, Ms. Taylor, I bow to your wisdom. I am but a mere neophyte when compared to your sagacity."

"Thank you, Mr. Barrymore."

"May your research go well, madam."

"May your work be rewarding. Please pass, sir."

Funny, thought John, *but after a while, this whole routine seems perfectly normal. Counterfeit reality?*

The bouncer passed into the main room of The Sunset. A new week had begun.

Pausing in front of the open kitchen window, in hopes of catching a glimpse of Molly, John Coyle experienced an unexpected, yet not unpleasant, pang of disappointment. The lady was nowhere to be seen. *She must be at the back working*, thought John. *She sure looked good Saturday night though.* He hoped to get a chance to talk to her before the night ended.

On his way to greet his employer, who was busily engaged in polishing a contentious stain on his otherwise gleaming mahogany, the bouncer noticed Delbert and, threw him the peace sign. The music maker responded in kind, smiled, and, flipped a switch on his high-tech amplifier. "Tequila Sunrise" sounded amazing!

By the time Mr. Coyle reached Mr. Kmetzko, the annoying stain on the bar had been eradicated completely. *Maybe Charlie'll be in a good mood.* John was kidding himself.

Without a semblance of greeting, Charlie broke into a tirade vociferous enough to force Delbert into cringing behind his massive sound system.

"Freakin' idiots! Is it too much to ask them to use a freakin' coaster? If it were their house, they'd use one!

No. Maybe I'm wrong. These freakers probably live in a pig sty! Ignorant jerks! Man, I'll tell ya, John, one day, I'm just gonna walk outta here! It's not worth the freakin' stress."

The bouncer attempted to placate his frustrated employer: "I know you're right, Charlie but, this place couldn't survive a week without you. Too many people depend on your leadership and guidance. Without you in command, these people would be lost."

John's words seemed to accomplish the desired effect. "Well, maybe you're right, John. It's just that sometimes it isn't easy being the head honcho." Mr. Kmetzko's voice was calm and subdued. Delbert's head could be seen peeking above his amplifier.

"I'm sure it isn't, Charlie but, nobody else could do it." John had a knack. "Hang in, boss. I'll talk to you later. Better see what Delbert is up to."

John raised his hand in departure and, Charlie began inspecting glasses for dishwasher stains.

The bouncer neared to within speaking distance of Delbert.

"Hey, big guy, what's happening? Glad to see you came out of hiding."

"Right on, man! Uncle Charlie can be one scary cat when he wants to be. I've learned to disappear when he trips like that. Better to hide than to be crucified."

"I can dig it." *When in Rome*…thought John.

The tall disc jockey continued: "Did you check out 'Tequila Sunrise' when you came in, man?"

"I did and it sounded fantastic!" exclaimed John enthusiastically.

"Yeah, I'm really starting to get turned on by these tunes. Customers seem to get off on the songs too. Do you have any more of this music, my man?"

"I can bring you some Beatles' stuff if you'd like." John seemed genuinely pleased that his music was appreciated.

"Beatles? I think I've heard of them but…"

"That's okay, Del. I know you're gonna dig these guys." John smiled. *Yeah, yeah, yeah, yeah!*

Because Monday nights were always debut nights at The Sunset, and, always unique, the club's guardian solicited a preview of events from the club's musical director. The inquiry had been perpetuated for years. "Anything new tonight, Del? Any ladies gonna become superstars because they danced at our little establishment?"

"Thought you'd never ask, my bench pressing Sheriff of The Sunset! Actually, we have a foxy new attraction who's supposed to be a groove to behold. Her name's Scarlet Flynn."

"What's so different about this lady, Del?"

"From what my uncle tells me, she's about 'the most beautiful and talented young artist we've ever hired.' She's booked for a month solid! I can't remember anyone ever playing here for that long. I even think ol' Charlie is paying her extra but, you didn't hear that from me."

John was impressed. "Well, she certainly seems like a heart breaker alright. I'm looking forward to seeing her."

Nine o'clock. Time for shadowing the shadowbox.

"Better get to work, Del."

"Okay. Cool. Catch ya later, John."

To Sleep, Perchance to Dream

The evening progressed without incident for Mr. Coyle. These were the kinds of shifts he preferred. By eleven twenty-five, he was almost bored.

The dancers had been more than adequate, the audience receptive and, Delbert had definitely found his groove.

John had been checking his watch several times over the last hour. He had been counting the minutes until Molly emerged from her station. He had been hoping she might be dressed in her black miniskirt. He had been scheming of clever things he might say to her. He had been contemplating how he might ask her for the pleasure of her company outside the realm of The Sunset.

The bouncer glared at his watch again. It was eleven thirty-nine. The dancers were running a bit behind schedule. Molly would be finished work soon.

At eleven forty-three, Delbert Kmetzko began his shtick: "Esteemed patrons of The Sunset Club, it is with great pleasure that I introduce tonight's special headliner! Tonight is her premier performance of an extended engagement. Please give a warm Sunset welcome to the lovely, Miss Scarlet Flynn!"

The spotlights dimmed.

The opening notes of something slow, with a solid bass line emerged from the club's extravagant sound system.

Soft, pastel colours gradually washed the stage in surreal combinations of red, yellow and, blue.

The lights intensified in value.

Lying prone, near centre stage, was the most exquisite female form John Coyle had ever beheld. She was perfect alabaster polished into divine inspiration.

As the music gradually increased in tempo, Venus arose from the depths.

Supple waves of crimson hair cascaded over delicate shoulders and framed a face of ethereal proportions. Sea-green eyes. A mouth hinting of a smile without really smiling.

The music crested and subsided and the dancer emulated each note. She never writhed around the brass pole but, touched it suggestively when the routine demanded intimacy. She never displayed the slightest hint of base or ignoble pleasures as she danced. She floated above the stage. She became part of the lights and music.

To John, The Sunset had always been a magical place but, with the appearance of Miss Flynn, the bouncer began to believe in Xanadu, Brigadoon and, Oz.

The music ended as it had begun.

The stage dimmed into blackness.

The dancer disappeared.

Spotlights flashed upon an empty stage.

Raucous applause filled the hall.

The spell was broken.

John Coyle had no comprehension of how long the performance might have lasted. It could have been hours. It might have been seconds. The concept of time meant nothing while the dancer worked her sorcery.

The enchantment had evaporated in purple mists of truth.

John Coyle was hurled back to his world of Sunset reality.

He inspected his watch. It was now twelve ten.

Molly must have departed by now. For John, the event didn't seem as important as it had mere moments ago.

There were nearly two hours left to work and more acts to appear but, to the bouncer, existing actualities of life meant little.

He wanted to be swept back in time. He wanted to once again be caught up in the dance, feel the music, taste the colours, and, paramount in his thoughts, he wanted to assimilate the unearthly charm of Miss Scarlet Flynn through every pore of his being.

Finally, the shift ended and, John Coyle was free to reflect upon the evening's moment of mesmerism without being fettered by the details and constraints of the responsibilities of his chosen profession.

Lying in bed a short time later, the stricken somnambulist couldn't remember leaving The Sunset or the walk home. Sleep eluded him for what seemed like an eternity. When he did succumb, it was with a smile on his face.

Heaven on a Hardwood Stage

When John awoke late Tuesday morning, he wanted to somehow will the hands on his watch and on his kitchen clock to spin insanely in a clockwise direction like a trite "time passes" technique of an old Hollywood movie. He wanted to be back in the main room of the Sunset at approximately eleven thirty. He wanted to repeat the previous night's dream.

Throughout the day, John Coyle forced himself to drift through the commonplace activities of typical existence. He ate, tinkered with the old Chevy, worked out and, washed some clothes at the camp's Laundromat.

By eight thirty, he set off.

A few minutes later, the bouncer was greeted by the lovely and convivial Ms. Taylor, benign Cerberus of The Sunset.

"Good evening, my young and famed orator! If my intuition holds true, I believe I detect a certain bounce to your step tonight and, the faintest of a propitious smile upon your comely visage. Have you perchance evoked your magic to procure the role of a lifetime, sir?"

"Ahh, were it so, Ms. Taylor. Alas, my humble attempts at simple prestidigitation equate to mere parlour tricks when compared to such wonders recently bestowed upon my mortal eyes!"

Ms. Taylor appeared momentarily confused but, would not relinquish the intent of the script. She would not deviate from her familiar persona. "Well, my good man, may you reap such marvels throughout your voyage of life. Please pass."

"Thank you, Ms. Taylor. I find myself once again in your debt."

Once John had passed through the turnstile into the land of shadow and light, he veered slightly to his right and encountered his employer busily engaged in taking stock of his bar's current liquor needs.

"Hi, Charlie. How's it going tonight? Everything okay?"

"Oh, hi, John. Yeah. I think everything is good to go. I've been thinking of ordering some more booze soon though. If that new dancer is as good as I think she is, the local stiffs are going to need a lot of freakin' drinks to cool down their temperatures!"

John blushed slightly.

Charlie continued. An imperceptible grin appeared on his thin lips. "By the way, John, where'd you get to last night? I was gonna see if you wanted a beer after work."

"Oh, thanks anyway, Charlie. I was a bit tired so I thought I'd get right home to bed. Mondays are always… umm…tiring."

"Yeah, you're right about that, John. Never know about Mondays." Mr. Kmetzko smiled openly.

"Oh, man, I just remembered something." John was anxious to get away before Charlie pressed on. "I'd better talk to Delbert. I promised to bring him some Beatles' tunes and I completely forgot. See you later, Charlie."

"See you later, John. Try and catch the new dancer if you have the time. I think you might like her." Charlie displayed very pronounced dimples when he smiled so widely.

A few hasty steps later, found the bouncer staring down at the top of Delbert Kmetzko's head as the announcer appeared busily engaged in cueing the club's sound system to play appropriate music between the dancers' sets. Delbert hadn't noticed John's arrival.

The amicable intruder cleared his throat.

Delbert responded with a salutation distinctly his own. "Yo, yo, yo, bouncing brother! Dig Del at work. Programming the electronic beast to kick out righteous sounds to soothe and rock the souls of the hip and square alike!"

"Cool, my man! Looking forward to getting into your rhapsody of rock." John hoped his words had some semblance to "Del-speak". "I have to apologize too, my man. I completely forgot those Beatles' tunes I promised to bring tonight. I'm really sorry. I know you're gonna dig 'Lucy in the Sky with Diamonds' when you hear it, Del. You're gonna be able to do some fantastic effects with the lights! It'll be unbelievable!"

"Sounds like a real trip, John. I promise to do my best. You bring the tunes and I'll spin 'em."

"Okay, my resident musical genius. I won't forget. Catch you later. Better stake out my territory."

"Right on, John. Later."

Tonight, The Sunset's guardian chose an area near the exit between the booths on the west side of The Playroom to begin his shift. He would move several times throughout the evening. Sometimes, the change in locale would be swift. Sometimes, the bouncer would linger at a table talking to patrons. Sometimes, he would lean on the polished bar and evaluate the behaviour of specific clients. Everything depended upon circumstances and the "feel" of the night. John Coyle tried his best not to make mistakes.

The bouncer's first real challenge of the night arrived at eleven minutes after eleven. Francine, La Femme Fatale had just finished her repertoire and had adjourned to the privacy of the spacious dressing room. She had performed well and, polite applause had followed her slow titillating exit.

A single patron, obviously drunk and, obviously enthralled with Francine's seductive moves refused to believe that the act had concluded for the evening. As he pounded his empty beer mug on the surface of the heavily lacquered table at which he sat near centre stage, the gentleman accentuated each blow with a loud, slurred bellow: "Bring back, Fransheen! She ain't done dancin'! Who said she could go? Get out here, Fransheen!"

The belligerent customer was a big man but, inclined toward fat. Maybe an inch or two shorter than the doorman. Fifty pounds heavier. Greasy mullet haircut. Sparse moustache. Red and black checkered jacket. Scuffed work boots. Dirty jeans. A bull with a beer belly.

John approached cautiously. It was far easier to defuse a potentially dangerous situation with finesse and cunning. Relying upon might and muscle could result in severe unpleasantness. *Be a matador*, John told himself. *Pick this toro apart with guile and skill.*

The bouncer pulled up a chair and situated himself directly across from Mr. Mullet. He spoke softly but, with authority: "Sir, my name is Coyle. I work here and I know for a fact that Miss Francine won't be repeating her act until tomorrow night. It's unfortunate because I know you really enjoyed the performance. What do you say I call you a cab? You can get some sleep and come back tomorrow night if you like."

"Call yerself a cab, buddy! I ain't goin' nowhere 'til I shee Fransheen!"

This latest tirade caught the attention of several customers who began to stare unabashedly at the noisome scene. A minor annoyance.

John leaned closer. "Okay, listen, mister. I didn't want to say anything because my boss told me to keep my mouth shut. You seem like a good guy though…a man who can be trusted. If I tell you something, can you keep it to yourself? Kind of a secret between two big guys who appreciate beer and fine women."

The bouncer had captivated the bull's attention.

"Huh? What're you shayin'? Make it fasht. Ain't got all night!"

"Alright, listen." The bouncer spoke in low esoteric tones. "Did you notice anything *unusual* about Francine when she was dancing?"

"Yeah, she was beautiful."

"I'm gonna be straight with you, big guy. Just keep it down when I tell you, okay?" John's brow tightened and his eyes swept the immediate surroundings. There was no one in earshot. "Did you notice how big Francine's hands were?"

"Huh? What the hell are you talkin' 'bout?" the aficionado of club dancing was confused but, at least, his voice was controlled.

John Coyle persisted. "Didn't you find it a little weird that Francine has an Adam's apple?"

"What're you shayin' for God's sake?" This time the bull's voice registered in the loud whisper range.

The matador withdrew his *espada*. "Okay, friend, I'll give it to you straight. Francine is really Frank. Sometimes, the lines get blurred in this business."

"Holy Jesus! How the hell was I s'posed to know? I never had no idea…"

"Don't worry about it, big guy. Nowadays you never know what you're getting. Not your fault. I'm sure not gonna tell anyone."

"Jeez, I really 'preciate that, man. Maybe I'd better get that cab after all and get some sleep. My eyes are prob'ly real tired. Thanks again, buddy for keepin' this between us."

"I've forgotten about it already. Nothing ever happened."

The two men shook hands to solidify their pact.

This time, the bull was spared but, Coyle had cut it close. There were only two minutes left until show time.

At precisely eleven thirty, Delbert Kmetzko began his carefully rehearsed spiel and, upon completion, pressed the appropriate button to free the music which would soon herald the arrival of Miss Scarlet Flynn.

Replicating the previous night's introduction, the low, hypnotic bass notes seemed to merge with the primary colours saturating the hardwood stage.

Tonight however, the routine differed in its opening venue. Tonight, three pale yellow spotlights illuminated the closed runway door. Moonbeams reflecting upon a portal to another world. The door slowly swung open. What emerged was liquid movement.

When the dancer reached centre stage, the music stopped abruptly and a single beam of blue bathed the vision in an eerie, subdued glow. Soft strains of violins permeated the atmosphere. She moved among the notes. Red replaced blue. Scorching synthesizer strains. The dancer became a flash of fire attracting all who beheld and, therefore, believed. Light dimmed. Pale greens and yellows. Acoustic guitars picked in harmony. She transformed into a wisp of smoke floating above waters in which mortals must surely drown. Darkness fell. Shards of silver above the sleeping lake. Daylight broke. The dream had vanished.

It took John Coyle several moments to regain his breath.

Molly's voice sounded somewhere in the proximity of the present and, the bouncer was abruptly reminded of his place in time. "Hi, John. That was a really different show, wasn't it? I think the dancer was fantastic! I caught most of the show since nobody seemed to be thinking of food when she was on. Delbert did a great job with the sound and lights too!"

"Yeah, you're right, Molly. That was some show. Better get going though. Still have a couple of hours ahead of me. See you later."

"Okay. See you later, John."

The bouncer turned and began a cursory search of a different vantage point. He hadn't noticed Molly's short black miniskirt or new shoes.

Delbert's Dimples

The following evening found John Coyle relinquishing two of his precious Beatles' tapes to an anxious Delbert Kmetzko.

Charlie had been absorbed in poring over paper and checking numbers with his vintage calculator so the bouncer's arrival had gone unnoticed by the cantankerous proprietor. John Coyle had seen no reason to disturb his employer's mental gymnastics.

"Okay, Del, here's the music I promised. I've got 'Magical Mystery Tour' and, 'Sgt. Pepper's Lonely Hearts Club Band' by The Beatles. Be sure to check out 'Lucy in the Sky', man. You're gonna trip!"

"Thanks, John. I'll be really careful with these, my man. As soon as I get some time, I'm gonna listen to each tune and rate it on my own coolness scale of from decent to far-out!"

"Right on, Del. Take your time. I think you're gonna dig 'em. Catch you later."

"Hang on a second, John. I was just wondering something. What do you think of the new dancer's trip? Personally, I think she's a groove!" When Delbert smiled that broadly, his dimples bore an uncanny resemblance to those of his uncle.

"She's good alright. She, ahh…seems to have something…umm…" The Sunset's custodian couldn't seem to find the appropriate response to a simple inquiry.

"Yeah, I thought that's what you'd say." Delbert's grin seemed to split his face. "Okay, chief, catch you later. Stay cool." The disc jockey flipped John the peace sign.

John mirrored the gesture and faded into the sanctity of The Playroom.

Song of Sirens

Something completely unforeseen and markedly altering befell John Coyle as Miss Scarlet Flynn completed her routine that night. As she approached the runway door, she paused briefly, glanced sideways and, for a fleeting moment, met the bouncer's eyes with her own. She smiled the faintest of smiles and retreated into the depths of her primordial lair.

That night, tigers with sea-green eyes inhabited the dreamscape of Mr. John Coyle. The tigers were lithe and predatory. The tigers were dangerous. The tigers were exquisite. When the beautiful cats purred enticingly, it was the song of sirens. Mr. John Coyle was lured into pouncing distance yet, he bore no fear. He had to touch the cats. He was compelled to become as one of them.

"The Girl with Kaleidoscope Eyes"

On Thursday night, Miss Scarlet Flynn, rising star of The Sunset Club abandoned the wooden stage of the main room in favour of a world of imagination centred within the walls of mirrored trickery and mortal deception. A dream within a dream.

With Delbert Kmetzko's extraordinary skill and unique application of modern technology, the hardwood stage of The Playroom was transformed into an image which, until now, had existed solely in the mind of a brilliant and prolific creator.

Scarlet Flynn had betrayed her earthly form and morphed into John Lennon's mystical "Lucy in the Sky with Diamonds". As the enigmatic tune from The Beatles' "Sgt. Pepper's Lonely Hearts Club Band" filled the shadowbox with dynamics propelled by pure imagery, it was "Lucy" who danced under skies laden with diamonds, not Scarlet.

Spotlights of "yellow and green" bathed the newly transformed stage into a wonderland of "cellophane flowers" and "tangerine trees" among which Lucy floated. The "girl with the sun in her eyes" glided over a landscape of magical bridges and mysterious train stations. Then she was gone.

In a flash of lightning, it was Scarlet who stood near centre stage with arms lifted skyward. The music had ceased. The colours had disappeared. The dancer seemed to be beseeching the gods of fantasy to delay her transformation. It was too late. They were unbending. They were steadfast.

As Miss Flynn slowly retreated down the carpeted runway toward the door to reality, she paused midway and meticulously scanned the room for a lighthouse to guide her steps. She found the bouncer transfixed on her own image. She ceased her endeavours and rewarded him with a look that penetrated John Coyle's very subsistence. He smiled. She coyly returned the gesture. He took a step forward. For the second time that evening, the lady vanished.

A Confrere's Confession

"…and last night, she turned and took a step toward *me* before she left the runway. This time, when we smiled at each other, I'm positive that everyone in the room was watching. I don't know, Mr. Spinelli, tonight, I think I'm gonna stand near the door when she finishes and introduce myself before she leaves the runway. What do you think?"

"What do I think, my friend? I tella you what I think. I think it is good to follow your heart inna such matters but, do not forsake the brain as you…pursue this inclination." When intent mattered, Mr. Spinelli chose his words carefully. "You wanna be careful."

"I know you're right, Mr. Spinelli and, you know I appreciate the advice but, it's just that every time I see her, I forget my own name."

Mr. Spinelli feigned a look of great perplexity. With a steadfast and solemn gaze, he spoke slowly and with authority: "Your name is John Coyle. Nobody ever call you 'Johnny'."

Both laughed.

Mr. Spinelli continued: "I know you know what is best for you but, is jus' I no want you to make same mistake as me."

"Same mistake as you? What mistake did you make, Mr. Spinelli?" John's curiosity had been awakened.

"I'll tella you, my friend but, first I needa little wine to keep throat good an'…cooperative. You care for some?"

"No thanks, Mr. Spinelli. I have to keep a clear head tonight." John thought that judging from the intensification of his friend's accent, that Mr. Spinelli may have already moistened his throat.

"I be righta back then. I bring the bottle out an' tella you a story."

Within a minute, Mr. Spinelli returned from his trailer with a bottle and glass, sat down from across his guest at the deck table and, poured himself a liberal dose of tongue loosener.

He began his story. "Like I tella you before, after terrible…demise of most beautiful an' lovely wife, I come to this country with mucha hope inna my heart.

"Turns out, I be lucky. I get good job right away with 'Panelli's Chinese Buffet and Take-Out Restaurant'. Luigi Panelli knew I like to drive so he often senda me out to very distant streets to deliver food. Driving givva me time to think. Also, tips good. I was still a younga man an' inna couple of years, I save enough for down payment of very small house way up at top of Steep Hill Road. Even had small garden. Very beautiful place inna country. Lotsa trees. No neighbours. I even buy a big dog for company. Life was good, my friend."

"Sure sounds like it, Mr. Spinelli. It must have been beautiful up there."

"Oh, it was but, it get even better! One day, I go to town to buy supplies. I stop at new grocery store to get veal an' ground up pork for meatballs I wanna make. When I go inna, I see beautiful an' lovely lady behind counter. She was quite plump with very good hips. The name onna her tag was 'Antonietta'. I buya many pounds of meat that day. I go back many times. Always I buya meat. Lotsa meat. Dog an' I start to gain weight. Is okay. Soon Antonietta an' I begin the dating. In six months, we...spoused!"

"That's amazing, Mr. Spinelli! You must have been quite the ladies' man. What happened next?"

Mr. Spinelli emptied his glass and poured another. He smiled and shrugged.

"Well, for next few years, all was most...domesticated. I worka for Luigi an' Antonietta worka at home. Is good. Then, slowly, things begin to change. Two people needa to talk about more than meat. Antonietta get plumper. I ask for more hours from Mr. Panelli. Is not...blissful.

"One day, Luigi senda me far out inna country to make delivery. Maybe fifteen miles past my own house. I get to door and knock. Nobody come. Knock again. Nothing. Who knows? Maybe people had to leave for emergency. Anyway, I start back to restaurant.

"Then, I get idea! What if I make slight detour an' drop off order at my house? Antonietta will be happy an' maybe we could talk. Maybe even act like honeymooners! Mr. Panelli always say that food is no good cold. Even on his van, the words, 'Hot Delivery Guaranteed!' be printed inna red.

"When I reacha my house, I was very...bewildered. There, inna my driveway, was Luigi Panelli's van! What could this be? I turn off car engine an' sneak up to kitchen window. There, on kitchen table were Antonietta an' Mr. Luigi Panelli! He was making a 'Hot Delivery Guaranteed!'.

"Slowly, I turn an' back away. My face was hot an' red. I feel like I wanna throw up. I lean against van of Mr. Luigi Panelli before I fall down. I stay downed for several minutes. Then idea come to me. I stay away from my own house for a little longer time. I have to think.

"Next, I throw open house door an' yell like crazy man: 'Get outta my house, you disgraceful, sneaky man of no virtue!' Even dog start to howl an' run out door. He almost knock me down! Well, Luigi Panelli follow dog most… hastily. Antonietta follow him. I no counta on this. I never think she go too! They jump inna van an', with mucha speed, get off my property.

"What can I do? I go to my car an' take out order of Chinese food. I go inside an' sit at kitchen table. It was already clear. I no believe my luck! Chinese food was still hot! This very terrible event of evening make me most hungry.

"I be almost finished moo goo gai pan when I hear sirens from somewhere down road. Sirens stop. I finish dinner an' break open fortune cookie. Fortune inna cookie say, 'Prepare for company.' I hope it no be Luigi an' Antonietta.

"About an hour later, I still be sitting at table. I am drinking a little red wine when I hear knock at door. When I open door a crack, inna run dog. I open door more an' see policeman standing there. Is my 'company'!

"Policeman tella me bad thing, John. He say that wife an' Luigi Panelli killed inna horrible accident at bottom of hill. He say something about van's brakes but, I be too… distraught to understand."

John Coyle was stunned by his friend's calamity. "I'm so sorry, Mr. Spinelli. You have suffered more than your share in life. I don't know what to say."

Mr. Spinelli poured himself more wine.

"Is okay, John. Everything worka out. During investigation, all sympathy go to me. My new friend, the policeman say he glad I no come home sooner an' see most unpleasant act of…indiscretion which he feel probably… transpired inna my own house. I no tella him any different. Would not change anything."

As Mr. Spinelli downed the last dregs of wine from his glass, John Coyle was *almost* positive that he detected the faintest of smiles appear on his friend's lined face.

No, don't be crazy. Poor old guy's just had some bad luck in life. His stories are probably greatly exaggerated too. Probably makes things up. Probably gets confused.

John Coyle valued Mr. Spinelli's friendship and, respected his opinions. Still, it might be an opportune time to graciously depart.

"Well, Mr. Spinelli, you certainly know how to roll with the punches. You're a remarkable man. I'm gonna get going though and get in a quick workout before my lettuce and cottage cheese. Tonight could be quite interesting. You enjoy the sun, my friend. I'll let you know what happens. If I don't see you tomorrow, I'll pop by Monday. Okay?"

"Sure is okay, John. Almost time for a nap anyway. The sun makes this old man feel like dog sleeping onna front porch."

I wonder whatever happened to the dog, thought John. *No way I'm gonna ask though.*

"Well, thanks for the advice and the story, Mr. Spinelli. It's always interesting talking to you. See you soon."

"You take care, my friend. Remember what Spinelli tella you. Take time to think."

"I'll try and remember, Mr. Spinelli."

John Coyle rose from his chair, shook his friend's hand and set off toward his own trailer to pick up his dilapidated gym bag. He hoped he could keep his mind on his workout.

First Words

Most of Saturday evening sped by in a surrealistic blur for The Sunset's monitor.

He remembered morosely discussing the current crop of Hollywood's elite with Ms. Taylor and arriving at the mutual conclusion that, for the most part, these new actors lacked substance and lasting charisma.

The bouncer visualized Molly as she greeted him through the kitchen's serving window but, the contents of the conversation eluded him. His mind was elsewhere. Nice smile though.

John recalled that Charlie Kmetzko had been "freakin' ticked off" with his nephew's insistence that the club was in dire need of a dry ice machine in order to enhance the dancers' art. The increase in the price of "freakin' peanuts" didn't help to mollify Mr. Kmetzko's sour disposition either.

Delbert had surpassed himself in striving for elusive sounds and unparalleled lighting effects. "Can you dig this,

John? What a trip it would be to have disco lights flashing to some of ol' Ludwig van's stuff! What a mind-blower, man!" John couldn't remember the technical aspects of the concept.

Hours passed. Nothing to interfere with or bend the laws of time or space. Patience on a temporal level must be rewarded with a glimpse of heaven if one were to believe in magic.

At fifty-two minutes past eleven, Miss Scarlet Flynn completed her final pirouette. This evening, the dancer had combined some classical ballet movements with contemporary pop songs. The resulting hybrid of both media equated to a breathtaking performance. The spectators expressed their approval in vociferous applause.

As the lady made her way down the runway toward the door leading to the stairs to the dressing room, she noticed John Coyle and paused before disappearing for the evening. She smiled at the bouncer. He smiled back and stepped closer to the runway. Miss Flynn veered toward the edge of the carpeted pathway to within speaking distance of Mr. Coyle.

Delbert Kmetzko played something soft in the background.

The Sunset's patrons lowered their voices.

"Miss Flynn, my name is John Coyle. I guess you could say that I'm the club's peacekeeper." John reached up and extended his hand.

Scarlet reached down and grasped it firmly. "Nice to get a chance to talk to you, John. I asked Mr. Kmetzko about you and, he had nothing but good things to say." The lady relinquished the bouncer's hand.

"Charlie's a good guy, Miss Flynn. He's really impressed with you and, to be honest, with the extra business you've brought in."

"That's good to hear, John. I try my best."

"I think you're the best dancer I've ever seen, Miss Flynn. What you do goes way beyond what anyone has ever done here. You could be performing anywhere with your talent." John hoped he hadn't spoken too impulsively.

"Those are very kind words. Would you do me a favour though?"

"I'd do anything, Miss Flynn. Just ask." John thought he might have spoken too impulsively.

"Please, don't call me 'Miss Flynn'. That sounds like I'm a wrinkled old librarian about a hundred years old." The dancer smiled.

"Okay, I promise. You sure don't look like any librarian I've ever seen either. You're beautiful." John was positive that he had spoken too impulsively. His blush affirmed his conclusion.

"Thank you again, John. You're very gallant."

The bouncer's face deepened two shades of red.

The dancer continued: "Right now, I'd better get off the runway though. Other girls are waiting to get to work. I could change and meet you at the bar in about twenty minutes. I don't think Mr. Kmetzko would be too upset if you fraternized with a fellow employee for a few minutes. What do you think, John?"

"I don't think that Charlie would have any problem at all, Scarlett. None at all. See you later."

Miss Flynn vanished behind the door.

Delbert Kmetzko cued the music for the next performer.

Charlie poured himself a shot of Southern Comfort.

John Coyle grinned sheepishly. His shoes seemed glued to the floor.

Well Worth the Wait

For the next twenty minutes, the Sunset's peaceful enforcer racked his brain for clever repartee, witty banter and scintillating discourse. His brain yielded nothing. He decided to stop thinking so abstrusely.

Finally, the object of the bouncer's contemplation had simply emerged stealthily through the deeply adumbrated runway door and descended the four steps leading from the start of the carpet to floor level. She had crossed over to the bar, claimed a stool and, had initiated a conversation with her employer and bartender, Mr. Charlie Kmetzko.

As John approached, he couldn't help but notice how pronounced Charlie's dimples really were when he smiled. Mr. Kmetzko was smiling a lot.

John pulled up the bar stool that his boss had reserved for him since the arrival of Miss Flynn and, positioned himself close to the dancer. He did not however, wish to infringe upon the engaging conversation taking place. A respectful smile and nod would suffice.

"What if you were to purchase the peanuts in bulk, Mr. Kmetzko? I imagine they'd last a long time in the shell and, they'd probably be a lot cheaper to buy."

Charlie raised his eyebrows and leaned over the bar to gain closer proximity to the alluring Miss Flynn. Because of his diminutive stature however, the effect was negligible. "You know something, miss? You might be right! I'm gonna look into your plan first thing Monday morning. Thanks for the great idea…and, please, my name is…Charles."

John Coyle raised *his* eyebrows. He also bit his tongue in order to suppress a laugh.

"You're more than welcome, Charles. I only hope things work out." Scarlet had completely captivated her employer. She smiled broadly to consolidate the facile accomplishment.

"Well, I'd better get back to work now. Take a break, John. If anything comes up, I can look after it." Charles puffed his chest out to the size of a large squab.

"Thanks, Char…les. I'll just be a few minutes." The bouncer sincerely appreciated Mr. Kmetzko's offer and his plucky spirit.

Charlie nodded and, swaggered down the length of the bar. Customers needed him.

"You know, I think he likes you, Scarlet." John's remark expressed more fact than opinion. He could see it in Charlie's face.

"I like him too, John. He seems like a pretty good guy, especially for a boss." Scarlet was sincere.

"Yep, he is."

"From what Mr. Kmetzko says, you're a pretty good guy too, especially for a bouncer." Miss Flynn smiled playfully.

"Well, not too bad I guess, especially for one employed in this allotted field." It was John's turn for a sportive rejoinder.

Again, Miss Flynn smiled.

Mr. Coyle decided to press on.

"I'd better get back to work, Scarlet. I wouldn't want to take advantage of…Charles' generosity. I was wondering something though. I know it's really short notice but, would you like to do something for a little while tomorrow? I could pick you up and we could just play it by ear."

"I'd love to do something tomorrow, John. I don't have anything planned at all. Would around twelve be okay? My apartment number is six. Just ring."

"That'd be great, Scarlet! I'll get to work now but, I'll see you tomorrow."

The bouncer rose from his stool, shook the dancer's hand and made his way several steps away from the bar. He turned around but, the lady with the green eyes had vanished.

John hoped the old Cavalier would start tomorrow.

Strangers in Paradise

On Sunday morning, at exactly eleven fifty-four, John Coyle parked his second-hand Chevy in the rear lot of The Sunset Club, near the back stairs. He was not alone. Occupying a spot five spaces away, sat a sixties Plymouth Barracuda convertible painted a brilliant orange. A broad white racing stripe stretched from dazzling chrome bumper to dazzling chrome bumper.

Seated in the front seat of the 'Cuda, one behind the wheel, one on the passenger's side, were two living concrete blocks. Each massive set of shoulders supported a freshly shaved head of equally large proportions. Necks were not visible. Two pairs of eyes were hidden behind dark sunglasses.

As John closed the door to his Cavalier and began the few paces which would lead him to the staircase, he nodded to the mountains. His gesture was ignored. *Must have skipped a good breakfast*, thought John caustically. *Maybe that's why they're cranky.*

A few seconds later found the courteous caller about to swing open the portal to the small entry room, when a tall gentleman burst forth, nearly battering John with the steel door. The stranger stood about three inches taller than John. His swarthy face was deeply pock-marked. Long, greasy strands of black hair were slicked straight back. Beady dark eyes completed the initial impression.

"Sorry, buddy. I wasn't thinking," uttered the startled departee. His darting eyes seemed to have great difficulty in making even a momentary contact with John's forthright gaze.

"No problem," responded John. "We didn't even dent the door." His attempt at levity was wasted.

The stranger's face took on an air of total indifference. "Yeah," was his reply. He stepped past John and finished his descent.

John assimilated more details. The man in a hurry was dressed in a garish floral shirt accentuated with red suspenders and a heavy gold chain. White slacks. Patent leather loafers. He seemed sinewy and moved with fluidity.

Mr. Suspenders hastily retreated to the orange 'Cuda and slouched down indolently into the back seat.

One of the concrete brothers ignited the beast and, the trio took wing.

Maybe they're going out for a good breakfast. The bouncer smirked at his own speculation. *That should put everyone in a better mood.*

A Most Auspicious Start

John shrugged, entered the inner chamber and pushed the buzzer announcing his arrival to "Occupant, Room 6". Almost immediately, a familiar voice responded to his summons.

"Hello. Is that you, John?"

John spoke directly into the circular wire mesh protecting the intercom speaker connected to room number six. "Yep, it's just me, Scarlet. Hope I'm not too early."

"No, no, you're right on time, John. Just give me a minute, okay? I'll be right there." To John, the lady's voice seemed somewhat flat. Somewhat devoid of enthusiasm. He hoped it could be attributed to the hollow sound of the communication system.

"Sure, take your time, Scarlet. I'll be right outside enjoying the sunshine." Actually, John wanted to make sure his old Chevy wasn't dripping oil. He had just topped up the tank that morning.

Just as Mr. John Coyle assured himself that the ancient Cavalier wasn't marking its spot too excessively on the club's tarmac, Miss Scarlet Flynn descended the adjoining stairs leading from the second floor and, soon found herself facing her unabashed admirer.

John spoke first. "Good to see you in the daylight, Scarlet. Hope you had enough sleep." The lady looked tired and distracted. The bouncer commanded himself to try harder. "Dancing looks like it could take a lot out of a person. You feeling okay? Rested?" *Quit while you're ahead,* he willed himself.

Scarlet smiled. John was glad she did.

"I'm just fine, thanks, John. It's just that it's rare for me to be outside this early on such a beautiful day. I guess I'm just not used to it."

It was John's turn to smile.

Scarlet was disarming. Simple jeans and a dark green T-shirt had replaced her inimitably designed stage apparel. Her thick hair was pulled back in a ponytail. Very little, if any, makeup enhanced her fine features. And, what secrets did her sea-green eyes possess?

John was grateful that Scarlet seemed to be awakening in the sunshine. He wanted to see her smile again.

"Do you like ducks, Scarlet?"

This time, the lady laughed. "Well, I don't know, John. I guess so. I've never really thought about it much. Do you always come out and ask questions like that?" She grinned.

"No, not all the time. I just wanted to see your face light up again. I am glad you like ducks though. Wanna go for a ride?"

"Sure," Scarlet replied, without hesitation.

Twenty minutes later, the pair pulled up along the grassy shoulder of a gravel road. Trees and overgrown shrubbery had replaced the streetlights and telephone poles of the city.

John threw on the emergency brake. The two stepped out of the vehicle.

"Where are we, John? I can't remember the last time I was in the country. It's beautiful here!" Scarlet now seemed relaxed and genuinely pleased to find herself a part of this new environment.

"I discovered this place about three years ago while I was killing time on a Sunday afternoon," John replied. "See that tree line over there? If you follow me, in a few minutes, we'll be standing right under a huge oak. That tree marks the spot that I visit whenever I have the chance. The path is a little more worn now but, when I first came here, you could hardly see it. I was curious about the old trees standing out there so I decided to stop and explore. Would you like to see a secret place, Scarlet?"

"There's nothing I'd like better, John! I'm just glad I'm not wearing my dancing shoes though. I'd never be able to keep up with you."

"Okay. I'll go slowly but, just be careful. You wouldn't want to sprain your ankle."

Scarlet looked concerned.

"I'm just kidding," John reassured her. "The path is actually pretty clear. I doubt if we'll see any snakes either."

"If we do, I'll be waiting back at the club for you!"

Scarlet and John soon arrived at their destination unscathed by treacherous rocks or venomous serpents.

John smiled as he watched Scarlet absorb the view for the first time. He was glad that he had brought the dancer.

Here, surrounded by densely crowded spruce, birch and, maple trees, a large, almost circular pond claimed its place as an oasis of teaming, vibrant life.

Hidden in recesses near shore, frogs croaked and, when startled, plunged under the thick canopy of protective lily pads.

Gregarious red-winged blackbirds emitted fluid gurgling strains as they darted among tall cattails. No single perch seemed ideal for very long. New vantage points had to be hastily explored.

Farther out from the bank, partially submerged fallen branches provided sunning platforms for sleepy turtles of all sizes.

Stretching out about eight feet from shore, an exhausted dock appeared ready to succumb to the ravages of time. Boards were missing and, several piles were slime-coated and appeared rotting. Still, the antiquated structure stood triumphantly. It had so far won its battle over gravity and the elements.

The towering, gnarled oak acted as sentinel over the hidden treasure trove. Its outstretched limbs shielded precious wonders from unwanted intruders.

It was while in the custody of the giant oak, that John Coyle and Scarlet Flynn exchanged glimpses and insights into each other's existence.

John spoke honestly yet sparingly. He answered questions when they were posed and, readily supplied details when he felt they were expedient. He spoke of minor annoyances and major compunctions. John relinquished painting the past in multi-faceted layers for the privilege of discovering the circumstances which had brought this breathtaking lady to his side in the present.

Scarlet, in this environment, free from affectation, found herself discussing details of her life which had gone unspoken for years.

The beautiful narrator spoke like she danced, precisely and fastidiously yet, as effortlessly as a stream of flaming magma. John could envision each chapter of her tale like a series of celluloid frames clearly delineating each scene. He listened without interruption as the film unwound.

Scarlet told John of a tranquil middle class upbringing in which she had enjoyed a loving relationship with her doting mother and hard-working father. Although the family never had money to squander, there was always enough for basic necessities and an occasional extravagance. Dance lessons, because of the inherent skill demonstrated by the young, Miss Flynn, were always considered a vital aspect of family existence, never a superfluous embellishment.

Things changed abruptly for Scarlet when she was fifteen. That was when her father died suddenly of a heart attack at the age of forty-two. The cohesion the family had once enjoyed had abruptly terminated. This was the time when the world stopped spinning.

Scarlet's mother seemed to lose her effervescence almost overnight. With each passing day, she became more depressed, quickly agitated and, more demanding.

Since Scarlet's father had been the family's sole source of income, new avenues of revenue now needed to be explored. Scarlet had quit her dancing lessons and had assumed a myriad of mediocre jobs in order to assist with expenses.

Her mother however, seemed too despondent to maintain a position of earning for any length of time. Nothing seemed to alleviate Mrs. Flynn's dark mood. Her spirit had been broken.

About a year after her father's demise, events seemed to take a turn for the better for Scarlet. She had, with some trepidation, applied for a modelling job which she had come across in the local newspaper and, had been granted an interview. The meeting was a great success except for one minor detail. Because of Scarlet's extraordinary looks and mature presence, the interviewer had assumed she was several years older. The young lady did nothing to dispel the notion. The job was hers.

Mrs. Flynn seemed pleased with her daughter's good fortune and had embraced Scarlet for the first time in many months.

For the next several weeks, Scarlet found herself juggling school with modelling jobs which never seemed quite as glamorous or lucrative as she had envisioned. Still, they were jobs. They helped.

Then ten days before her sixteenth birthday, Miss Flynn was presented with an unexpected opportunity by her agency. If she would relocate to "the big city" about three hours to the north, the fledgling fashion devotee would be guaranteed the remarkable sum of seven-hundred dollars a week. Board and transportation would also be provided. Intimations of even bigger opportunities and paydays were dropped. It was the chance of a lifetime that couldn't be ignored.

Little discussion was required between mother and daughter. Scarlet would accept the job. School would be put on hold. The money was of paramount importance. Much of it would be sent home.

Two days after her sixteenth birthday, Scarlet began her quest to live out her fortuity. She embraced her mother and boarded the waiting taxi. Bright lights and a better life beckoned her.

Seventeen days after her sixteenth birthday, Scarlet demanded what she thought was fair recompense for her time and trouble and walked out of her questionable "modelling" contract. The bright lights of fame and fortune turned out to be grimy, out dated spotlights illuminating talentless automations sleepwalking their way through badly written perverse scripts.

With little money and nowhere to stay, Scarlet realized that some source of steady income was a life-sustaining necessity.

Within two days, employment was attained. Dancing in The Imperial Room of The Lakeport Inn and Tavern six nights a week paid living expenses with some money left over to send home. For a moderate cut of her weekly cash settlement, Scarlet was leased a small, but clean room in which to live. The cash was good and, Miss Flynn's skill level at her new profession increased nightly.

Two months of promissory work stretched into five months of steady concrete reimbursement. Money was sent home. Money was saved. Bright lights had become a reality.

When The Imperial Room began a two week period of renovations, Scarlet decided it was an opportue time for a visit home. She hadn't seen her mother in months and was anxious to touch base.

With a single valise resting at her feet on the front porch, young Miss Flynn knocked at her mother's door with great anticipation. The ride home had been long and tedious and, Scarlet was anxious to see her mother. She knocked again. Finally, activity could be heard within. The sound of footsteps grew louder and the door at last swung open.

Scarlet was shocked at how old her mother had become. She was also shocked at the smell of alcohol on her mother's breath. Once Scarlet had been invited in, mother and daughter embraced briefly and soon found themselves seated at the kitchen table catching up on events of the past several months. Scarlet sipped coffee. Her mother sipped brandy.

About forty minutes into the conversation, a loud, slurred bellow emanated from the vicinity of Mrs. Flynn's bedroom: "Colleen, have you seen my damned wallet? I gotta go out and get some smokes."

"Come on out here will you, Ray? There's somebody I'd like you to meet."

Scarlet was taken completely by surprise by her mother's offhand request. No mention of any type of gentleman companion had been cited throughout the dialogue, nor had the topic been broached during previous telephone conversations.

Ray soon appeared. He was fiftyish, balding, overweight, of medium stature and, in dire need of a shave. His undershirt was stained and, his jeans required the attention of a gifted seamstress. His grey socks may once have been white.

As he approached the kitchen table, Mrs. Flynn delivered the introductions: "Ray, this is my daughter, Scarlet. Scarlet, Ray."

"Nice to meet you, Scarlet," asserted Ray as he extended his hand. "Your mum never told me you were this pretty."

As Scarlet haltingly accepted Ray's outstretched hand, she noticed his breath reeked of cigarette smoke and beer. She also noticed that his handshake was a bit too firm and lingering. Miss Flynn withdrew her hand hastily from his sweaty palm and muttered a quick nondescript salutation.

"Ray, Scarlet is going to stay over tonight so that we girls can catch up some more. You will stay won't you, dear?" Mrs. Flynn appeared genuinely pleased that her daughter was there.

Ray's yellow-toothed grin affirmed that he too was delighted with the lovely guest.

"Well, just tonight, Mum, if I won't be causing anyone any bother. I have to be back tomorrow for an interview." A small deception meant to satisfy her mother. A falsehood meant to extricate herself from an uncomfortable situation.

Once Ray had disappeared on his quest to appease a habit, the two women resumed their conversation. Except for the superfluity of spirit imbibing on Mrs. Flynn's part, the talk had been pleasant and informative.

At twelve ten, Mrs. Flynn stumbled to her bedroom.

At twelve twenty-seven, Ray emerged. He had previously retreated to the lair when cigarettes had been obtained.

At twelve thirty-one, Scarlet slapped Ray's face with all the force she could mobilize.

Ray slithered back to the confines of the bedroom.

Scarlet summoned a taxi and promised herself to phone her mother at the soonest opportune moment.

"…and, that's just about it, John. I've been dancing ever since."

Clickety-click, clickety-click. The projector in John's mind had allowed the last of the film to detach itself from the still spinning reel.

"Well, personally, I'm glad you continued to dance, Scarlet. If you didn't, I'd never have met you. Besides, you're too pretty to sell vacuum cleaners." *Think before you speak*, the bouncer enjoined himself.

"Vacuum cleaners! Where did you get that from, John?"

"I don't know, Scarlet. I think things just kinda escape my mind sometimes."

Both laughed.

Both sat in the shade of the oak and silently observed life unfold at the oasis. Neither felt it was necessary to mar the moment with words.

Finally, it was John who broke the trance. "Scarlet, I don't even know how long we've been here but, I'd better get you back. I don't want you to get too bored with me all at once. I was hoping I'd get more chances."

Scarlet laughed, reached over and, squeezed John's hand. "John, I've had a great time. I'm sure not bored with you or this beautiful place. I hope you'll bring me again soon."

"That would be my pleasure, Scarlet. Next time, I know we'll see some ducks!"

John smiled.

John smiled broadly on the drive back to The Sunset.

John smiled very broadly when Scarlet kissed him on the cheek before disappearing behind the door of apartment number six.

A Heart Beating Strongly

When John Coyle pulled up at his trailer a few moments later, he was still smiling.

Deciding that he wanted some time to himself, the bouncer chose to forego a visit to Mr. Spinelli and indulge himself in events which would allow his mind to replay the afternoon's experience in vivid detail. Tomorrow, he would call on his friend.

After partaking of a thick tuna salad sandwich, a large crisp dill pickle and, a frothy protein shake, The Sunset's security man grabbed his battered gym bag from the bedroom closet, filled it with freshly laundered apparel and, set off to exercise his body. Physical routines had become ingrained but, vigilance had to be maintained. Still, during lulls between sets, there would be time for visceral meandering.

Since his heart seemed to be beating exceptionally vigorously, John Coyle elected to work his chest. According to the bouncer's mental schedule, his pectorals were due for the workout.

Beginning with light bench presses, John gradually increased his poundage and variety of exercises until he was ready to work his way down in weight and gradually cool off. He always employed strict form. A torn muscle was not advantageous to his chosen profession.

After nearly two hours, the bouncer was exhausted. The workout had been intense and rewarding. He had concentrated on the movements but, had still envisioned Scarlet's face with every repetition performed. He couldn't help it.

The first thing that John did when arriving home a few moments later, was to indulge in a long refreshing shower.

The second task was to withdraw a frosty beer from the fridge and indulge in a long, refreshing drink.

That evening, while sitting on his deck and gazing at the stars, the bouncer imagined "Lucy" once again dancing among the shimmering diamonds. She never danced better.

Later, while lying in bed waiting for sleep to override his churning emotions, John deliberated upon another Beatles' tune. In "I've Just Seen a Face", the face belonged to Scarlet. She never looked more beautiful.

Three Strikes but,
Never Out!

"And that's about it, Mr. Spinelli. All I can say is that tonight when I go to work, I hope she'll want to see me again. I just can't seem to get her face out of my mind."

"Well, John, I'm jus' an old man but, inna my life, I have had a few…liaisons with most beautiful an' lovely women. I tella you this so I have the…credibility to offer opinion. You sure you no like something to drink?"

John looked at his watch. "No, thanks, Mr. Spinelli. I have to be at work in less than two hours. You go ahead though."

Mr. Spinelli rose from his deck chair and entered his trailer. In a moment, he returned with more red wine. He poured himself a large goblet and sipped appreciatively.

"Okay, John. I tella you something in order to … illustrate…forthcoming point. After Antonietta…depart,

I live for several more years inna old house with only dog for company. Of course, job with Panelli finished for good. By now, I'm no longer younga man. I am most fortunate though because I now do the work for Gino O'Reilly, a good man who own construction company. I worka witha concrete when Gino require me. I am very lonely though. Meet no most beautiful an' lovely ladies. Dog jus' sleep all day.

"One day, I get idea! I write to Uncle Donatello inna ol' country an' explain to him my…dire circumstances. By the way, John, Donatello translate to 'Given by God' in the English. I wait with breathless bait for his reply.

"Inna one month, I receive letter. It brought great joy to my heart! Uncle Donatello write that inna one month more, I go to city and withdraw beautiful an' lovely woman from train station. She givva consent to marry me! Her sweet name is Arabella. In English language, 'Answered Prayer'. I be so happy I wake up dog an' tella him good news. He snort, roll over an' go back to sleep. I coulda tella he be happy though.

"Finally, big day arrive. I go to city an' find train station. Dog stay home an' sleep. Inside station, I look around. Only one person inna room. She seated on bench with two suitcases beside her. The suitcases were very large, John. I… surmised that they contained very large clothes.

"Next, I walk up to lady, introduce myself an' ask if her name is Arabella. I fear the worst. The worst come true. Arabella was her name. She was not my 'answered prayer'.

"The lady stood up an' offered hand. I shake it. The hand was very…corpulent. The lady smile at me. Her lips were also corpulent. I stand back an' look better at her. Arms. Legs. Everything very corpulent. She look like short, round salami dressed inna black casing. Under my breath,

I curse Uncle Donatello. The lady no speak English. She probably think I offer up prayer for her arrival.

"What to do? What can I do? Nothing. I must behave with honour. We leave station. Before going home, we stop at Justice of Peace. He marry us. I have no ring but, promise one in the future. I know it will be a corpulent expense.

"Once home, Arabella prepare dinner. It was most excellent! I should have known.

"Bedtime arrive too soon, John. Because I try... assiduously to be gentleman, I will say only this: I was not the man I thought I was. I make little impression upon her...appetite. Is okay. She fall asleep soon. She snore most loudly. Dog wake up frightened. I let him out. I never see him again.

"Days pass. Arabella becoming most demanding. I worka hard at construction company jus' to put food on table.

"Weeks pass. She make more demands! Bigger refrigerator. More shelf space. New stove. I become tired of extra hours I worka for her.

"Soon, first year of marriage arrive. Even more demands. Now she musta have cold cellar to store food she musta preserve.

"I begin the work inna basement. I worka at night. I sleep on cot. Peaceful. No hear snoring. Soon the work is finished. I ask Arabella to inspect. She does. She complain that room is too small. Why there is doorway but, no door?

"I go crazy for a while, John! My mind go blank! Next thing I know, I realize where I am. I not understand though why entrance to cold cellar is now blocked in. Cement work is excellent! Arabella is nowhere to be found. I begin to worry. Maybe she go for walk. I wait all night. She no come back. I wait days. No Arabella. Still, is not so bad. Plenty of food. Very quiet. Only worka when Mr. O'Reilly needa good cement man. Life become very…tolerable. I stay inna house ten years before I move here, John. I still miss dog though." A whimsical look appeared briefly on Mr. Spinelli's lined face.

A flash of incredulity broke upon Mr. Coyle's countenance.

"So, Arabella never returned, Mr. Spinelli?"

"No, my friend. She never come back. Marriage never seem to worka outta for me."

Well, at least I know what happened to the dog, thought John.

Mr. Spinelli drank heartily and continued. "Remember, John when I tella you that you no Superman an' you can be tricked?"

"Sure, I remember, Mr. Spinelli."

"Well, my friend, here is the moral for you. Beautiful an' lovely ladies may not be what they seem at first impression. Sometimes, ladies not…free buffet!"

John Coyle suppressed a grin but, with the requisite tone, responded to his friend's well-intentioned counsel. "I'll remember your words, Mr. Spinelli and, always try to look at beautiful and lovely ladies when my stomach is full."

"Well said, John! I salute you!" Mr. Spinelli drained his glass.

Onions, Peanuts and, Dry Ice

Monday began Miss Scarlet Flynn's second week of employment at The Sunset Club.

That evening marked the end of Mr. John Coyle's first week of replete enchantment and plenary devotion to the lady with the sea-green eyes.

After a fleeting discussion concerning the relative merits of studio contracts, the ever-knowledgeable and, always scintillating, Ms. Taylor allowed the debonair and intensely personable, Mr. Barrymore to enter freely into the land of smoke and mirrors.

Passing by the open window of the club's kitchen, en route to the bar where Charlie Kmetzko seemed busy heaping large translucent red bowls with peanuts, John Coyle was disappointed that the alluring face of Molly could not be discerned in the hingeless casement. He paused and peered in. The bouncer spotted Molly, in profile, at the large built-in wooden chopping block sunk into the kitchen counter. She was busily engaged in dicing onions with a small cleaver. Molly was dicing with a vengeance. She was forceful beyond necessity. She chopped with the precision of a starving surgeon on commission. Something about the way Molly sliced through the succulent bulbs made John Coyle wince. He decided to greet her with respect and considerable restraint. He decided to employ just enough volume to be heard over the sharp, whacking cries of the cleaver.

"Hi, Molly."

Molly paused long enough to sink the tip of the cleaver's blade into the cutting board deep enough to lodge the instrument securely. She turned briefly to John. "Hi, John." Her face was devoid of its usual warmth and charm. Her tone was cold. Molly pivoted, pulled the cleaver free and resumed her frenzy. Her passion for the task seemed to mount.

Maybe she just doesn't like onions, thought Mr. Coyle as he quickly took his leave.

I hope Charlie's in a better mood.

Mr. Charlie Kmetzko did indeed appear in jubilant spirits as he greeted John a moment later. "Evening, my boy! How ya doin' tonight? What d'ya think of the new décor? Pretty classy, huh?"

The Sunset's ramrod was certain that his employer must be referring to the new, large bowls brimming with roasted peanuts that were spread evenly along the glistening bar within easy reach of every thirsty customer. There had been no other discernable changes in The Playroom as far as John could tell.

"The bowls look great, Charlie but, aren't they awfully big. It'll cost you a small fortune to keep them filled every night, boss."

"Not so, my young friend! Because I listened to our new star attraction, I now buy in bulk! I have huge burlap bags filled with freakin' peanuts piled up to the ceiling in the storage room! The peanuts come already salted right through the freakin' shells! Imagine that! The more I buy, the cheaper the price. Our clients will gobble these goobers up and become thirstier and thirstier. The thirstier they get, the more they drink. The more they drink, the more profit we make! That Miss Scarlet is a genius. I shoulda thought of this before! Buy in bulk, John. That's the freakin' key!"

Throughout his animated discourse, Charlie Kmetzko's pasty complexion had transmuted from white to pink and, from pink to crimson. His employee feared that a stroke was certainly forthcoming.

"Whoa, Charlie! Slow down, boss! Remember, peanuts alone can't bring happiness." John's snippet of homespun philosophy seemed to greatly appease the bartender. Within seconds, Charlie had returned to his chalky old self.

"You're right, John. I guess I just got carried away for a minute. The thought of gettin' out of this freakin' business a little sooner gets my blood boilin'."

"Well, you take it easy tonight, Charlie. I'll meander over to Delbert's station and see what he's up to. See ya later."

"Yep. See ya later, John." Charlie grinned impishly and began topping up the peanut bowls.

As John neared Delbert's castle of sound, it was evident that the younger Kmetzko was also in a celebratory mood. Like uncle, like nephew. A jocular jockey. Before John could offer up a greeting, the young tunesmith fired off a verbal barrage of alacrity that would fell most men. John Coyle was tougher than most men though. He stood tall against the onslaught. "John, John, how are you, my man? You're looking very cool! Work out today? You're never gonna believe this, brother but, Uncle Charlie Cheapskate told me that I could buy any dry ice machine I dug! Said if I thought it would benefit the club, then I should go out and get it! Far-out! He said something about peanuts too but, I didn't catch his rap. My uncle's the best, man! I'm going shopping tomorrow. Unfreakin' believable! What do you think, John? Too much, huh?"

"Yeah, way too much, Del but, if the man gives his blessing, then go for it! He's the boss."

"Yeah, right on, John. It's just that it's not like him to be so generous. Oh, well, this is gonna be a mind-blower!"

"Can't wait to check out your new toy, my man. I know it's gonna be a trip and a half! Better get to work now though. Kudos, my friend!"

"Thanks, John. Catch you later. Got some last minute stuff to attend to myself. Freakin' job ain't easy ya know."

John raised his hand and scanned The Playroom for his first vantage point. He departed when he was satisfied with his choice.

The Return of Mike Murphy

The next couple of hours passed slowly and uneventfully for John Coyle. He checked his watch. He mingled. He checked his watch again. Finally, he could count the remaining minutes on one hand until the presence of Miss Scarlet Flynn would fill The Playroom.

At exactly eleven twenty-six however, the bouncer's wistful daydreams were suddenly cut short by a vociferous entreaty shot from Charlie Kmetzko. The detonation arose from the vicinity of the bar. "John, get over here fast! There's someone in big trouble!"

Dodging tables, chairs and, people, the doorman converged upon the source of contention within seconds. At the front of the bar, a very rotund gentleman was gripping the back of a stool with one hand while wildly gesticulating toward his throat with the other. The gentleman's face was beet-red. He was stomping the hardwood floor with his right foot. The gentleman was choking.

As John drew nearer, he realized that he recognized the man. It was Mike Murphy of "Murphy's Meats". The bouncer immediately took charge of the situation. "Okay, Mr. Murphy, you're gonna be just fine. I'll have you fixed up in a few seconds. I'm coming around the back of you now. I'm gonna join my arms around the bottom of your diaphragm, make a fist, give you a good abdominal thrust and, dislodge whatever is cutting off your air supply. Nothing to worry about, okay?"

"Ahhh…" Mr. Murphy made a raspy noise.

"Okay, get ready, Mr. Murphy!" John tried to wrap his arms around the meat monger. His hands fell several inches short of making the proper connection. He tried again. The results were the same.

"Ahhh…" Mr. Murphy made another raspy noise.

John responded quickly. Time was vital. "Charlie! Get over here! Give me your right hand!" Charlie responded quickly. The bouncer grasped Charlie's right hand in his own left. "Now," John continued, "we're gonna circle Mr. Murphy right here and I'm gonna make a fist with my right hand. Grab it with your left. Got it?"

Charlie understood. "Freak!"

Instructions continued fast and furious. "Okay, let's tighten our arms up a bit. Good. On the count of three, pull in quickly and firmly on my fist. I'll do the same. Okay?"

"Freak!"

"One…two…three!"

The manoeuvre worked splendidly.

What spewed forth from Mr. Mike Murphy's cannon-like throat was a conglomerate mass of half-chewed peanuts cemented together with hastily masticated pickled kielbasa purchased at Charlie Kmetzko's own bar!

The attending projectile came to rest in a large bowl of salty treats.

The bartender moved quickly to dump both container and contents into the garbage receptacle behind the bar. "Freak!" seemed an appropriate utterance when the task was completed.

Once Mike Murphy had regained his breath and composure, the first act of a grateful survivor was to thank Messrs. Coyle and Kmetzko for their altruistic labour.

Mr. Coyle was gracious in accepting Mr. Murphy's profound appreciation. He was also gracious when introductions were made between his employer and the proprietor of "Murphy's Meats".

When Mr. Murphy asked Charlie if there were anything he could do to possibly repay the debt, Mr. Kmetzko reflected for a moment and asked: "Do you happen to sell kielbasa in bulk, sir?" Charlie was not as gracious as John.

Once the crowd, which had gathered to witness the choking event had dispersed, John glanced at his watch once again. It was eleven thirty-one. The entire episode had lasted scant moments.

The lights dimmed. Strains of hypnotic drum beats filled the room. Scarlet stood poised on the runway, her beauty illuminated by a single blue spotlight.

The dancer looked directly at John, smiled innocently and, pressed the palms of her delicate hands together as if in preparation for prayer. She cocked her wrists and rested her head comfortably on the angle. The lady sighed and whispered with great exaggeration, "My hero!"

John blushed slightly, returned her gaze and, pantomimed his own supplication. "Tomorrow?"

That night, Scarlet Flynn levitated mystically above the runway as she swayed to the pulse of ancient drums impregnated with synthesized minor chords.

That night, John Coyle could feel his blood pounding like primordial earth-rhythms long after the music had faded into the void of the preternatural.

Sand and Snow

On the Tuesday afternoon of Scarlet's second week of her extended engagement at The Sunset, the dancer and the bouncer found themselves seated around the table on John's deck thoroughly engrossed in a discussion revolving around the relative merits of trailer living compared with apartment dwelling or rental habitation.

John thought that he had presented several valid points in favour of his present living arrangement and, was ready to summarize his contentions. "So you see, Scarlet, I have everything I need right here plus, I have a home base. I own my place outright and I'm free to keep it or sell it whenever I please." John seemed content with his closing remarks.

"Well, when you put things in that perspective, John, I suppose I see your point. It must get pretty barren sometimes in the winter though." Scarlet's last innocent statement seemed more like a question to her verbal sparring partner.

"Sure, it's a bit dreary during the winter, Scarlet but, spring seems to come around every year."

Scarlet smiled. "Have you ever pictured yourself sipping wine on the veranda of a little villa in Tuscany during a blizzard in December, John?"

"I have to admit, I could learn to appreciate that image."

"A Margarita on a beach in Mexico wouldn't be too bad either, especially around January, would it?"

"Not bad at all, Scarlet."

"Personally, I'd take a nice condo surrounded by palm trees and sand over just about anything else, wouldn't you, John?"

"I sure would, especially when I'm buried up to my axles in snow!"

Scarlet smiled again. Slyly.

John realized that the lady was a very persuasive orator. She had trapped him as easily as Mr. Spinelli had during countless games of checkers.

"Okay, you got me, Scarlet. I concede. I'd rather be living in an apartment on the beach any day!" John bowed in a gesture of resignation.

"I'm just kidding around, John. Actually, I really like your place. If I didn't have to move around so much, I bet I could get used to something like this. Florida would be nice though."

Both laughed.

Light conversation ensued for the next hour or so until it was time for John to drive Scarlet back to the club for a four o'clock rehearsal. Scarlet usually preferred to practise her routines in the late afternoon so that she could partake of a light dinner and rest before her scheduled time to perform. She readily agreed to accept diverse times however, since the rest of the dancers also had their preferences and individual needs to accommodate. Scarlet was the headliner but, she was no prima donna.

It had been a good afternoon.

A Smokin' Routine

As eleven thirty approached that evening, John Coyle realized that he was about to witness something very unique. Judging from Delbert's lopsided, just-wait-'til-you-see-what-I've-just-done smile and, the new, yet barely noticeable equipment delineating the runway, the bouncer knew that unparalleled magic was about to unfold.

He was not wrong.

At exactly eleven thirty, Delbert Kmetzko proclaimed the advent of The Sunset Club's main attraction: "Esteemed patrons of The Playroom, it is with great pride that we now present a lady with fire in her every step and a smile that melts hearts. Presenting…Miss Scarlet Flynn!"

Clamorous applause filled the main room but, Miss Flynn failed to appear. The door leading to the runway remained closed. The applause gradually subsided. The crowd grew silent.

It was the cue that the sound technician was hoping for. House lights were dimmed. The runway was set afire with the glow of blazing red spotlights. Smoke from obscured sources arose from the runway and billowed to near-ceiling level. The narrow stage assumed an eerie look of purgatory, softened by the forgiving hand of God Himself. A slashing series of guitar chords cut through the mist. John Coyle recognized the distinctive opening riff of "Smoke on the Water" by Deep Purple, the popular British band of the seventies. Appearing simultaneously, a plasma-like form seemed to greedily inhale the chord progression and writhe with fluid agility to the tempo. The dancer was a demon/angel with alabaster skin draped in red chiffon. Her sea-green eyes seemed to shine with an unworldly luminescence. Many in the audience broke forth with applause. Many gasped audibly. Others sat in spellbound silence. The music continued. The dancer matched every forceful rhythm and rock-solid beat with intense moves and creative manoeuvres born in the nether regions of her imagination.

As the song ended, a slower beat was layered over the fading notes and, a key change overpowered the Deep Purple classic. Delbert had worked his own technical wizardry.

Now, the mood became more passionate as the music grew sultrier. A moist heat replaced searing flames. The dancer had become vulnerable and human. She was capable of pain. As she enacted "Smoke Gets in Your Eyes" by The Platters, everyone in The Playroom believed that it was the dancer whose plaintive voice cried out woefully about abandonment and tears when "a lovely flame dies".

As soulful harmonies grew soft, Delbert skilfully blended music and meter forming a transition which was smooth and unhesitating.

The next piece was more up-tempo and seemed to evoke a feeling of vulnerability tinged with resolution. Scarlet danced like an angel but, not *too* angelic. Green eyes clouded in sorrow but, red chiffon flew in defiance. John recognized the song as "Smoke From a Distant Fire" but, couldn't recall the artist.

More music and fragments of tunes rounded out the dancer's time segment. All spoke of fire and passion, smoke and, tenderness.

The performance ended much like it had begun but, with greater excess in theatrical achievement and auditory extravagance. Thick, blue smoke, completely enveloping the dancer, now pushed against the ceiling tiles. A single synthesized chord, which could be felt churning in the stomachs of the patrons, bounced off The Playroom's walls.

Then, in an instant, with the flick of an invisible switch, the world changed. Smoke dissipated. Spotlights died. House lights proclaimed normalcy.

The audience sat in stunned silence. Several seconds passed before clients were able to express their sonorous acclamation.

Mr. Delbert Kmetzko had exhibited technical brilliance.

Miss Scarlett Flynn, in eurhythmics, interpretation and, spontaneity had been inspired.

Mr. John Coyle had fallen hopelessly in love for the second time in his life.

Watercress Wednesday

"I've never been here before, Scarlet but, it just seemed like the kind of place you might enjoy. Judging from the way you dance, I know you can't be fuelled on ribs and barbecue sauce."

Scarlet smiled at John's well-intentioned compliment. "The menu looks really interesting, John. I know this'll be great."

The bill of fare at "The Karma Carrot" was not renowned for its succulent steaks or butter-drenched lobster. Instead, only culinary offerings which were organically certified and grown by vigilant and conscientious nurturers were presented.

It took Scarlet and John more than a few minutes to decide upon their orders. Neither wanted to rush into something too exotic. In the interim, each ordered a tall glass of chilled pomegranate and celery juice to stimulate the palate. The juice was...well chilled.

Scarlet ordered first. "I think I'll have the spinach salad with sun-dried tomato bits and whipped tofu and vinegar dressing."

The young, emaciated waitress with algae coloured hair seemed genuinely pleased with Scarlet's selection of repast. "Excellent choice, miss! Our spinach is picked fresh daily!"

The lady in attendance now turned her attention to John. "And you, sir. What may I bring you today?" Her pen was poised.

John hesitated momentarily, then seemed to gain confidence. "I'd like the steamed alfalfa sprouts with a side order of shredded kelp and a pot of Chinese tea, please."

The waitress stared incredulously at John. "Are you sure, sir?"

"Well, yes…I think so."

"Very well then, sir." The lady with the verdant hair jotted down John's order, spun hastily, and marched through the swinging double doors into the kitchen.

Once safely hidden from earshot from paying customers, the waitress relinquished her orders to an equally thin, older woman busily engrossed in peeling a large papaya. The waitress confided her frustrations to her fellow restauranteur with a sense of profound disbelief. "You won't believe this, Hazel but, some guy at table three just ordered Chinese tea with shredded kelp. God, what was he thinking? I wouldn't recommend that combination to the owner of this overpriced joint!"

Both laughed as if only they were privy to appreciating the absolute folly of the gentleman from table three.

When the roughage arrived a few moments later, both Scarlet and John were equally impressed with the myriad of shades of green with which a healthy dinner could be imbued.

After picking at their palettes of chlorophyll-laden fodder for several minutes, while uttering the expected platitudes of approval, the daring connoisseurs' ardour for culinary adventure was quickly assuaged.

Scarlet began to giggle. John quickly followed suit. Honesty of palate prevailed.

John was the first to verbalize his disenchantment. "Scarlet, I don't know about you but, if I eat any more of this stuff, I'm gonna grow long ears and start raiding Elmer Fudd's carrot patch!"

"You're wight, you wascally wabbit! Let's depart this westaurant and gwab thomething a bit more thubstantial!" Scarlet knew her cartoons.

Twenty minutes later, the misguided gourmets pulled into the parking lot of "Chico's Fries and Extreme Burgers" with joy etched upon their famished faces.

After stationing the old Chevy as close to Chico's trailer as possible, John took Scarlet assuredly by the hand and led her to the "Place orders here!" window of the carnivores' haven.

"John!" exclaimed the proprietor, as he saw his friend and long-standing customer approach. "How are you doing, amigo? Haven't seen you for a while."

"I'm fine, Chico. Just been a bit busy."

The two men shook hands through the open window.

"Chico, I'd like you to meet Scarlet. Scarlet, this is Chico, the best in the business!"

"Nice to meet you, Scarlet."

"You too, Chico."

Again, the proud owner extended his hand, this time, with far more gallantry. It was readily apparent by the slight blush on his face and lopsided grin that Chico had already fallen under the spell of Miss Flynn.

"Well," continued Scarlet's latest admirer, once he had regained some composure, "what can I get you two kids? You look like you could use some real food."

"Man, you don't know how true that is," confirmed John with a nod. "Do you think you could rustle us up a couple of your famous 'Mucho Burgers', Chico?"

"No problem, my friend!"

"Does that sound okay with you, Scarlet?" asked John as he turned to his rapacious companion.

"That sounds wonderful, John!"

"Care to try some of Chico's 'Mega-Tub-o'-Fries'?"

"I'd love to, John!"

"What would you like to drink, Scarlet? Chico makes great 'Supreme Shakes'."

"Maybe just a diet soda, please, John. A girl has to watch herself you know." Scarlet smiled.

Minutes later, the dancer and the bouncer sat in the sun at one of the wooden picnic tables situated around the fry stand. Their feast was indeed a mucho, mega delectation.

Hours later, at The Sunset, despite their notable caloric consumption, Scarlet Flynn danced like an inspired sylph.

John Coyle kept the peace. The bouncer was very anchored.

Fast Franklin's Fabulous Flea Market and Richly Retro Emporium

As John Coyle pulled into the one-way roadside entrance of The Sunset Club on Thursday afternoon, he was jolted into spontaneous alarm as he gaped at the familiar, vintage Barracuda barrelling down on him from the opposite direction. The car was making fast headway, with tires squealing, as John, at the last moment, cranked the old Cavalier off to the right shoulder and braked hard, barely avoiding the orange missile. Stones flew as the convertible fishtailed onto the highway and disappeared. Tweedledee and Tweedledum had been jammed into the cockpit while Mr. Lank-and-Greasy rode shotgun in the rear seat.

Once John had regained most of his composure, he started up the stalled Chevy, inched back onto the asphalt and, swung left into the club's back parking area. Scarlet was descending the stairs. John parked the Cavalier.

"Who the hell are these idiots, Scarlet?" John demanded as he approached the dancer. "This is the second time I've seen them around here." The doorman was immediately sorry that he had been so abrupt. Scarlet looked as if she were about to cry. Still, he wanted an answer.

Standing face to face with John, Miss Flynn collected her thoughts. "They're people I've known for a long time, John. I don't want to know them anymore. I made that clear to them. Please trust me, John. It's you I want to know better, nobody else."

"Okay, look, I'm sorry, Scarlet. I do trust you and, I want to know you better too. It's just that I'm a bit protective toward my Chevy. It's a classic you know."

A faint grin appeared on Scarlet's face.

John decided to press on. "Scarlet, I was just wondering something. Have you ever been to 'Fast Franklin's Fabulous Flea Market and Richly Retro Emporium'?"

Scarlet laughed openly in response to John's innocuous question. "No, John, I've never been there! Believe me, I'd remember!"

"Great! You're in for quite an experience if you'd care to accompany me, young lady."

"I'd love to, John!" Scarlet stretched up and kissed John solidly on the mouth. "And thanks for being such a big teddy bear," she added when the kiss ended.

The drive to "Fast Franklin's" took about half an hour. Small talk and light banter occupied the thirty minute trip. Nothing was said concerning the unsettling incident of the kamikaze 'Cuda.

After parking and paying the two twenty-five cents admittance fees, Scarlet and John passed through Franklin's squeaking turnstile and found themselves standing at a very long corridor about eight feet wide. A hand-painted sign, resting on a wooden tripod at the starting point of the passageway, informed the couple that their point of departure was AISLE ONE. Made sense. An endless procession of cluttered cubicles lined each side of the smooth concrete path. Each booth was equipped with heavily laden shelves packed tightly with every conceivable treasure known to humanity. Proud vendors scrupulously watched over their hoards of prizes yet, vociferously entreated passers-by to help lighten their cache for a reasonable cash settlement.

John, although he had visited "Fast Franklin's" on several previous occasions, was still enthralled with the circus-like atmosphere which permeated every square inch of the vast arena.

Scarlet, a novice shopper, was completely awe-struck by the sheer volume and variety of available trophies displayed so openly.

Clutching John's arm tightly in hers, Scarlet appeared impassioned with the idea of undertaking a new adventure with her handsome and chivalrous guide. "Oh, John! This is great! I've never seen anything like this before! It's amazing! Thank you." For the second time that day, Scarlet kissed John. The kiss was passionate. The kiss lingered. John Coyle seemed to momentarily lose consciousness.

When the embrace ended, and John regained a modicum of actuality, he acknowledged Scarlet's appreciative remarks with his own gracious observation: "I'm the one who should be thanking you, Scarlet. You make me feel like someone special, somebody better than what I'll ever be. I couldn't wait to see you today."

The dancer gazed intensely at the bouncer. "You're my big teddy bear!"

John smiled and added: "I don't mind being your teddy bear at all but, I think you'd better lead the way.

My legs are kinda rubbery. Feels like I've just come out of hibernation."

Scarlet smiled, took John's hand and, began their quest.

Three hours later, the adventurous couple stood outside Scarlet's apartment door examining their priceless finds. For Scarlet, John had purchased three garishly coloured feather boas and a denim miniskirt encrusted with silver sequins and red rhinestones. John thought the attire might prove beneficial in future dance routines. For John, Scarlet had discovered and obtained a huge blue velour teddy bear and a black T-shirt with a picture of Rocky Marciano, poised for battle, emblazoned on the front. Both treasure hunters were thrilled with their gifts.

The dancer and the bouncer embraced briefly. No words were spoken. Touch and looks spoke far more than words.

Scarlet disappeared behind the door of apartment number six.

John set out for home.

Both knew that in a few hours, this present reality would vanish within the confines of The Sunset Club. Both understood the plurality of their inherent natures. They were role players, often by choice, sometimes, through necessity.

A Sojourn with Mr. Spinelli

As John and Scarlet approached Mr. Spinelli's site the following day, both were slightly apprehensive about the reaction they might elicit from the venerable sage. John wanted his old friend to like and accept Scarlet. Scarlet sought Mr. Spinelli's trust and understanding.

"Hello, John! Please come up an' sit! I see that today we are graced witha the presence of most beautiful an' lovely woman!" Mr. Spinelli rose from his chair on the deck and motioned the couple to join him.

Both took a step up. Two paces brought them face to face with their benign host.

John proceeded to initiate introductions. "Scarlet, I'd like you to meet my friend and checkers mentor, Mr. Spinelli. Mr. Spinelli, my…Scarlet Flynn."

"Nice to meet you, Mr. Spinelli. John has told me many good things about you." Scarlet displayed a smile accentuated with perfect white teeth.

"The pleasure is mine, Miss Flynn. John has also spoken of you inna most…laudatory fashion." Mr. Spinelli smiled. He still possessed many of his teeth.

An even score.

The bouncer seemed pleased.

"Please, sit down, younga people. The day is growing warm."

John and Scarlet pulled up chairs around the table which was shaded by Mr. Spinelli's green, white and, red deck umbrella anchored through a hole in the middle of the table.

"Now, my friends, what may I offer you? Inna refrigerator, I have the wine, beer an', poppa soda. I can also make, with no inconvenience, coffee or tea."

"If it's no trouble, Mr. Spinelli, may I have some ice water please?" Scarlet did not want to appear too demanding.

"Of course, my dear! Is no trouble. How 'bout you, John? Many hours before you worka."

"Okay, thanks, Mr. Spinelli. I guess one beer wouldn't hurt."

Mr. Spinelli rose and retreated within his trailer.

In whispered tones, John and Scarlet assured each other that the initial first few moments of the visitation had gone well.

In less than no time, the convivial host returned with a tray of refreshments, including the traditional bottle of chilled red wine from which he looked forward to imbibing. Socializing could be strenuous work.

After serving his guests, and pouring himself a small tumbler of his personal libation, Mr. Spinelli raised his glass and toasted his company. "Salute! To you, John and Scarlet!"

In response to the gesture of cordiality, John raised his beer bottle and, out of admiration for his old crony, presented his own token of respect. "To you, Mr. Spinelli! Thank you for allowing us to share this beautiful day with you. Also, from the bottom of my heart, thank you for allowing me to win the occasional game of checkers."

The three laughed and clanked bottle to glasses.

"So, younga lady, tella me something, please. How you like working with this big fellow? He is very…robust but, inna his occupation, he musta…exert vigilance at all times. Sometimes, I tella him that he no Man of Steel but, I betcha at the work, he sometimes come pretty close." Mr. Spinelli could be quite direct. His age afforded him certain liberties.

Scarlet smiled and reflected briefly before speaking. "You're right, Mr. Spinelli. John is the best there is. Everyone at the club, employees and guests alike, respect and depend on John more than they sometimes admit. He's tough but, more than that, he's extremely intelligent. He'd rather rely on his wits in a difficult situation. He's also very sensitive, as I'm sure you know. John can literally carry some obnoxious drunk outside, then, give a taxi driver money out of his own pocket to get the guy home safely. To me, Mr. Spinelli, John's more than a bouncer. He makes me feel good about myself. He makes me feel safe. He may not be Superman, like you say, but, he's a very special person as far as I'm concerned."

Outwardly, the big man blushed.

Inwardly, he was overcome with humility.

A sip of beer helped to open his suddenly constricted throat.

"Yes, you are right, younga lady! You describe my friend with mucha…succinctness. I never say these words to him for fear his head grow to size of small planet!" Mr. Spinelli possessed a verbal style distinctly his own.

The ancient host and his beautiful guest once again touched glasses.

John smiled. He was no planet but, Scarlet was the epicentre of the world. He was content to bask in her vitality.

The next two hours passed quickly and pleasantly. The three spoke of music, dancing, grape cultivation, the individual merits of several past heavyweight boxing champions, world politics, Renaissance art and, cartoon characters.

John had another beer and Scarlet accepted a glass of red wine.

No matter how cordial the gathering though, Mr. Spinelli's visitors had other commitments to fulfill. Scarlet had to rehearse and John had a week's worth of laundry to which he had to attend.

As the bouncer and the dancer rose to depart, each expressed sincere thanks to the generous and urbane host of the afternoon.

Mr. Spinelli smiled and bowed slightly. He expressed his own delight with the visit and asked his guests to return soon.

As Scarlet and John were about to descend the step leading from Mr. Spinelli's deck, the venerable gentleman halted his young companions with a simple request. "Please, Scarlet, may I ask you a question?"

"Certainly, Mr. Spinelli. Go right ahead."

"Thank you." Mr. Spinelli paused. "I have curiosity for… your esteemed opinion. Do you believe that the gentleman standing here can be tricked?"

Mr. Spinelli peered directly into Scarlet's sea-green eyes.

She returned his gaze with steadfast resolve.

An instant of complete understanding passed between the two.

John Coyle knew he was not privy to this mystical link. He was an outsider. He accepted his position. He stepped off the deck and walked several paces down the narrow road until he was out of earshot. He waited.

Finally, the lady spoke. "Let me preface my answer with a few thoughts first, Mr. Spinelli. I think there have been certain events in each of our lives which we have never discussed with John. Am I right?"

"Yes, you are correct." Mr. Spinelli's eyes remained unwavering.

Miss Flynn continued. "I don't think that means we are necessarily deceitful or trying to intentionally harm John. I simply believe that there is no reason to dredge up unpleasantries which may hurt him. He doesn't deserve more hurt in his life."

Mr. Spinelli nodded.

Scarlet continued. "So, to answer your question as directly as possible, yes, I think Mr. John Coyle can be tricked. He can be tricked because he is an open and trusting person."

"I believe that you help...clarify my own thoughts, Scarlet. I also believe that you an' I, maybe not so bad people. Maybe, we jus' make a few bad choices along way. Maybe we coulda be better if we try to look outta for Mr. John Coyle whenever time is...opportune. Do right thing for him." Mr. Spinelli smiled.

Miss Flynn reciprocated despite a fine film enveloping her eyes. "You're a very wise man, Mr. Spinelli."

"An' you are most beautiful an' lovely lady."

The two conspirators hugged warmly.

John noticed the embrace from his vantage point. He now felt convinced that the visit had been a great success.

When Scarlet joined him a moment later, John was eager to learn of her reaction to the afternoon's sojourn.

"What'd you think, Scarlet? You seemed to hit it off with Mr. Spinelli."

"I think he's sweet, John. Bright too. I really like him. There's just one little thing though." Scarlet cast her eyes downward.

"What's that, Scarlet?" Her companion suddenly seemed dismayed.

"When you first introduced me to Mr. Spinelli, you could have told him that I was your girlfriend." The dancer raised her face and smiled.

The bouncer kissed her passionately. The kiss lingered.

A Somewhat Large
Puppet on a String

That night, at The Sunset Club, The Playroom's gentle enforcer could not seem to linger in one spot for too long. He was agitated in an uplifting fashion. Kinetic energy with a grin. A mobile marionette.

During the carefully construed routine of each performer, John Coyle would inevitably discover several bars of music which seemed to compel him to move to the beat. Often, the bouncer seemed to be inventing his own rhythms and tempos which were heard by him alone. What the big man lacked in skill, he made up for in creativity.

There were times, when the music was so alluring, that John would even attempt to sing along to the dancer's recorded tunes. Key and pitch meant little to the maestro. The interpretation was what really mattered.

Charlie Kmetzko couldn't help but witness snippets of his employee's innovative manner of performing. "What the freak?" was his sole and, understandable reaction.

When Scarlet took command of the stage at eleven thirty, John's matchless gyrations and unprecedented vocalizations ceased abruptly. He did not want to appear a dancing teddy bear. Still, the grin persisted.

Slightly Distracted

Upon awakening Saturday morning, John realized at once that the day would evolve into an important pivotal point in his life. It would either result in a major compunction or in a glimpse of paradise. Everything revolved around one question.

As he prepared breakfast, John Coyle thought about the task ahead. How could he broach the subject? What words could best express his intentions? So many factors to consider.

John also ruminated upon the importance of fire prevention. As his trailer filled with thick smoke, the result of his failure to remove charcoal slices from the old-fashioned manually operated toasting appliance, John was pleased there was a gentle breeze wafting outdoors. With the door and window slung open, it really didn't take that long to air out the trailer. Perhaps a good omen.

Later, in the gym, the bouncer was blessed with another bit of good luck. As he stumbled away from the forty-five pound plate that *someone* had neglected to return to its designated place, he was thankful that his toe wasn't broken. In a couple of hours, he would *probably* be pain free. As John lifted the heavy weight back to the rack, he was pleased that his limp was barely perceptible.

Dinner proved almost uneventful. The chicken burger at "Chico's" was delicious! It took John very little time to change a flat tire on the old Chevy's rear wheel. The spare was inflated and the jack worked flawlessly.

At around eight, John shaved closely and hopped into the shower to ready himself for the night's activities. He wanted to be fresh when arriving at a personal crossroad a few hours in the future. The ice-cold water proved most refreshing. John would have to take a look at the hot water heater tomorrow.

Time to depart. The Sunset's resident arbitrator decided to walk. The sudden downpour had little effect on his hopeful spirit.

A Question of Monumental Reverberation

"Good evening, Ms. Taylor."

Ms. Taylor smiled and nodded from within the confines of her business station. "Good evening to you, my good man."

"Please forgive my audacity, madam but, do I detect a magnificent and, may I add, tastefully opulent new bauble you sport on your delicate finger?"

"Oh, Mr. Barrymore, you are always so observant and so generous with your praise! Yes, the ring is a gift from a very talented young man who happens to share our thespian interests. Though more comfortable interpreting the work of the great Mr. Shakespeare, I predict that one day, he will meet with renowned commercial success."

"I wonder, Ms. Taylor, might this fine gentleman be conversant with the work of Mr. Dylan Thomas? Might his genealogy arise from Wales?"

"Sir, you are indeed a well-informed scallawag! No matter how diligently you attempt to charm me however, a lady must always employ discretion when discussing delicate matters of the heart."

"Of course, you're right, Ms. Taylor. For some reason, tonight finds me playing the part of an optimistic imp hoping to glean positive replies from each query I pose."

"Could it be, Mr. Barrymore that you have a specific question of some magnitude which may be haunting your thoughts?"

"I yield to your enlightened perception, Ms. Taylor. Perhaps, if you would kindly allow me to pass, I might find some diversion in work."

"Certainly, sir. Before you commence your travail however, allow me to attend to a paltry bit of business which is marring your perfect profile." Ms. Taylor stepped from her post.

Mr. Barrymore seemed momentarily confused.

Ms. Taylor withdrew a lace handkerchief from somewhere in a recess of her ticket booth and dabbled at a speck of congealed blood on the gentleman's chin. "Nothing but a shaving nick, Mr. Barrymore. You men and your vanity."

Mr. Barrymore passed through the turnstile and became Mr. Coyle.

As the bouncer approached the open port of Molly's kitchen, he decided to test the young lady's reaction to a pleasantly delivered salutation. He hoped that her disposition had improved since the last time he had greeted her. Poking his face into the serving window, John nearly collided heads with the pretty cook as she attempted to peruse The Playroom's present clientele capacity. "Jeez, I'm sorry, Molly! I just wanted to pop my head in to see how you were doing."

"That's okay, John. No harm done." Molly turned and picked up the cleaver from the kitchen's cutting board. In a cold, sardonic voice, she turned to John and added, "I'm fine, John. I hear you've been really busy."

Before the bouncer could reply, Molly once more averted her face and began attacking a large Spanish onion with her glistening cleaver. Molly attacked with a vengeance.

This lady is really passionate about her work, thought John. He wanted to maintain a positive attitude.

As The Playroom's peacekeeper approached his employer's station behind the bar, he noticed that Mr. Kmetzko, like Molly, also wielded something provocative in his hand. Upon closer examination, John determined that it appeared to be a large, generously packed, unctuous looking sausage. Scanning the bar, Mr. Coyle was able to make a positive identification. On the bottom shelf, in front of the mirror and, behind Charlie's walkway, six large jars were placed approximately two feet apart. Each jar was labelled: "Mike Murphy's Meats". Below each commercial label, a hand-printed rectangle of paper was taped. In black marker, the message, "Kielbasa, 75¢" was printed.

"Hey, John! Try some of this. It's freakin' delicious! Way better than the stuff I used to sell! Mr. Murphy sells me the kielbasa wholesale. I practically double my profit on every jar I sell!"

Charlie Kmetzko's exclamations of avaricious joy took precedent over a more traditional greeting.

"It looks good, boss but, I think I'll pass. Thanks anyway though."

"What's the matter, John? Afraid to get a little garlic on your breath? Got a date after work tonight?" Charlie cackled at the cleverness of his own humour.

John smiled and shrugged. "Hope so," he replied as he sauntered away.

Delbert was next in line. John was always impressed with the ways in which the young audiophile tried to expand the club's innovative sound and light show.

"Greetings, Del." John aimed for simplicity.

"Greetings to you, John! What's happening, my man?" Delbert could sometimes express a clarity of intent.

"Nothing really, Del. I was just hoping for a preview of tonight's festivities. Any of the dancers rehearse anything new today? You know. Leave the people with a big impression."

Delbert thought for a moment. "Big Bad Bertha wanted to do something with an inflatable swimming pool but, Charlie didn't dig the trip. Said the water would make the carpet 'freakin' soggy'. Wasn't keen on ducks in the club either. Fanny Shaker and I practised a funky thing with strobe lights today. Could be pretty cool if she keeps her balance. Oh yeah, and then there's our headliner. She's too much! How she gets her ideas is a mystery to me, man. She puts my head through every night. Tonight, she's doing something from the groovin' sixties. A little Joplin. Some Grace Slick. Should be a trip, man. She even has some of those feathery things they used to wear. Far-out! You wouldn't happen to know where they came from would you, big guy?"

The bouncer smiled and nodded. "Okay, you got me. I give up. How come everybody around here knows so much?" John posed his question in the spirit of comradeship.

"Well, my friend, I guess it's because…we just love our big ol' bundle of joy!"

John laughed. "I'm gonna man my post now. The wackos and winos never give me as hard a time as you guys!"

"Okay, John, but try to relax. Miss Flynn will be on before you know it! Peace!"

John cordially returned the gesture of harmony and slowly made his way across the floor. He hoped the time would pass quickly.

Thanks to two bickering elderly ladies who both had illusions of romance directed at the same white-haired gentleman, a pitcher of beer which was inadvertently spilled on the lap of an off-duty police officer by a novice waitress and, an imaginative drunk who insisted that he was the illegitimate son of Truman Capote, time appeared fleeting.

At eleven thirty, Scarlet Flynn claimed the stage of which she had become the rightful heiress. Her routine of only twenty minutes managed to encapsulate an entire decade. Through her movement and interpretation, the lady painted a picture of optimism and hope. She expressed experimentation in life. She expounded upon music, fashion and, philosophy. She allowed the audience to visualize colours of a bygone and, perhaps, simpler era. The lady was brilliant.

As Scarlet took her leave of the sixties, John managed to raise his voice above the clamour of the crowd. "Scarlet, meet me at the bar after I'm finished, okay? There's something I'd like to ask you."

"Anything for you, my cuddly teddy bear!" Scarlet blew John a kiss.

John felt like he owned the world.

Hours later, as the last clients departed, John Coyle leaned against the bar and feigned interest in Charlie Kmetzko's enthusiastic review of the evening's accrued profits. "I'm tellin' you, John, what with the peanuts and pickled sausage, I'm makin' a freakin' fortune! I can see myself in Florida before much longer!"

"Well, I'm happy for you, boss. I hope you catch some big ones." The bouncer knew that Charlie would never abandon his theatre of improvisation.

John felt a tap on his back. He turned and was rewarded with the sight of Scarlet's resplendent smile.

"Hi, John." The dancer kissed the bouncer's cheek.

"Hi, Scarlet. Have a seat."

John pulled out a stool for her.

"Good evening, Charles. I hope you had a great night!" Scarlet liked her employer and wished him success with his every endeavour.

"Yes, miss, if I had more nights like this, I'd be livin' like a freakin' king in the beautiful sunshine state."

"Maybe one day soon, Charles. Who knows?"

"Yeah, you're right. Who knows? Right now I know I'd better tally up some numbers. See you kids later."

Scarlet and John uttered appropriate responses.

Charlie made his way to the cash register. He chuckled as he walked away.

John claimed a stool beside Scarlet and sat in silence. He attempted to form a mental strategy but, failed. Several more plans also met with abysmal results.

At last, John faced the object of his timidity and spoke. "Umm, Scarlet, I was just wondering something…"

"Yes, what is it, John?"

John meditated before answering. "Would you care for a beer?"

"Sure. That sounds good. Thanks, John."

The gracious servitor withdrew behind the bar and, seconds later, reappeared carrying two frosty bottles of Corona.

"Here we are, Scarlet. Nice and cold. One of the perks of the club. Free beer after work." John handed Scarlet a bottle.

"Thanks, John. Now what were you going to ask?" Scarlet took a sip of beer.

Again, John appeared lost in contemplation. He quaffed deeply from his bottle.

"Would you like a glass, Scarlet?"

"No, this is fine. Thanks though."

"Okay then. Here goes. We've been seeing each other every day and I think we've got something special going on. What do you think, Scarlet?"

"I think you've summed things up perfectly, John." There was no hesitation in Miss Flynn's voice.

Mr. Coyle continued. He tried to select his words with care. "Well, what I'm trying to say is that I think I'm... probably...I'm pretty sure that I love you."

"I feel the same, John."

The big man breathed an equally big sigh of relief.

He continued, hoping his luck would hold. "You don't know how good that is to hear. I was kinda thinking that maybe tonight you could come home with me. We can just see how it goes. I could drive you back here tomorrow. You could pick up some of your things or you could choose to stay in the apartment. It's up to you, Scarlet. I don't ever want to pressure you. I just want to keep seeing you."

The dancer leaned closer to the bouncer and whispered: "Let's go home, John."

"Yeah. Let's go home, Scarlet."

A Major Compunction

After a leisurely breakfast Sunday morning, it was mutually decided that John would drive Scarlet back to apartment number six. Clothes and personal belongings would be packed and the couple would then return to the trailer to set up housekeeping.

Since Scarlet still had two weeks left at The Sunset Club, plans for the future could be made in a fairly unhurried fashion. One day at a time. The present was good.

John was like a little boy with a secret he had to reveal before he exploded. Since it shouldn't take too long to move, he looked forward to visiting Mr. Spinelli and sharing the good news. He would buy some good wine and turn the event into a celebration. Scarlet and Mr. Spinelli seemed to hit it off well. The afternoon would be perfect.

As John manoeuvred the old Cavalier into the back lot of The Sunset Club, he noticed that he and Scarlet were not alone. Parked in the first row, in a space near the stairs, was the orange Barracuda. Two familiar forms occupied the second step leading to the dancers' living quarters. A third slumped over the railing. All three stared malevolently at the occupants of the Chevy as it drew nearer.

Scarlet gripped John's right arm tightly. "Keep driving, John. We can come back later. They're bad people. We should stay away from them." The lady's voice quivered. She sounded afraid.

"Don't worry, Scarlet. We're here to pick up your things and that's what we're gonna do. We can talk about these guys later."

John pulled the Chevy into a parking space a few feet from the Barracuda and threw on the emergency brake. He stepped out of the driver's side and made his way around the front of the car to open the door for Scarlet. "Come on, Scarlet. It's fine. We'll get your stuff and then buy some wine for Mr. Spinelli."

Scarlet exited and took John's arm. She remained silent.

As the two approached to within ten feet of the stairs, it was the tall, oily man who fired the first volley. "Good to see you, Scarlet. Been keeping busy? Me and the boys miss you."

John continued to lead the lady closer to the stairs.

Scarlet grasped John in a vice-like hold.

The couple reached the front of the stairway.

"Excuse us, gentlemen but, we have to get up here." The bouncer tried to use diplomacy. Sometimes it worked.

The granite brothers rose but, made no attempt at acquiescence. They turned to their leader for instructions.

Instructions were delivered. "'Fraid that ain't possible, buddy. These boys don't move for nobody. Maybe if you'd just go your own way, and leave Scarlet with us, then you won't have to get hurt."

John stared at the speaker with open distain. "That's a very generous offer, scumbag but one I just can't accept. Here's one for you though. If these little playmates of yours don't move in five seconds, I'm gonna break one of their noses. I'm not sure which one though. They're both equally ugly." The bouncer knew that he was entering territory that he found extremely repugnant but, he had no other choice.

To Scarlet, John whispered: "Go stand by the car, Scarlet. The keys are in the ignition. If anything happens, just get out fast."

Scarlet slowly retreated. She was crying.

John watched her leave. He smiled.

John turned and faced the two giants. His face remained a picture of felicity.

With lightning speed, and the force of a two-hundred, twenty pound sledgehammer, the bouncer struck Tweedledee squarely on the bridge of his broad nose. John felt bone splinter. Blood immediately gushed forth. Tweedledee bent over in pain. A hard right uppercut brought the monster to his knees.

Instinctively, John raised his left hand for protection. He dropped his chin. He knew that Tweedledum would immediately launch a vengeful, raging attack. The bouncer assumed a boxer's stance and mentally prepared to rearrange the second hulk's features.

The growling slab of anger rushed John. He wanted to crush the smaller man into lifeless oblivion.

The bouncer cocked his right fist.

John fired but, never felt the blow connect. What he did feel was something heavy and rigid crash down, with intense force, upon the back of his skull. He knew that he was bleeding profusely. He felt the blood streaming down the back of his neck. Fighting to maintain his equilibrium,

John turned to face his new adversary. The tall man stood poised with a pipe of considerable length and diameter. The weapon had been concealed on the asphalt, adjacent to the stairway. Greaseball was laughing hysterically, ready to strike again. John threw a left but, it glanced off the lanky hyena's chin, causing no real damage.

While the bouncer's back was turned, Tweedledum drove a cannonball fist into John's right side. The bouncer stumbled. Searing pain shot through his rib cage. He willed himself to remain upright. John Coyle pivoted to his right and caught his opponent solidly on the ear with a good left hand. Tweedledum winced in agony.

John lost his balance and began to topple. His descent was abruptly arrested by an enraged Tweedledee who caught John around his chest and swung him around like a rag doll. The blood from the broken nose of the behemoth dripped into the gash in the bouncer's head. Blood intermingled. Bad blood.

Tweedledee twisted John's arms behind his back. John could feel his left shoulder dislocate. His head slumped. Tweedledum and his slimy keeper now took turns at inflicting more pain upon their hapless victim. After countless blows, John Coyle could no longer distinguish between fist or pipe. He was growing numb. His legs had lost feeling.

Just before John lost consciousness, he glimpsed the man with the pipe drop his weapon and withdraw something from his pocket. The bouncer heard a metallic snap. Through swollen eyes, he saw the glint of the narrow blade of the stiletto.

The bouncer realized that his ordeal was far from finished.

John felt his body being dropped to the asphalt. Blackness overcame him.

Down but, Not Out

John Patrick Coyle's diagnosis was grave, his condition woeful. Still, he survived. He clung stubbornly to life.

The bouncer had sustained a severe head trauma, four cracked ribs, a dislocated shoulder, multiple contusions, a broken cheek bone and, lacerations to his face and chest requiring two-hundred, twenty-one sutures. The attack had been vile.

For seven days, John Coyle drifted in and out of consciousness. Reality became blurred. There were occasions when he writhed in pain and wished to die. There were times when he danced with a beautiful luminescent spirit under the starry skies of a van Gogh painting.

John, on several occasions, thought that he had been visited by characters who seemed vaguely familiar yet, somehow distorted, as if inked by a mad cartoonist.

One such spectre appeared as a wrinkled, yet kindly old soul, who seemed to enjoy board games and animated story telling. A macabre tale, focussing upon the accidental death of an unfaithful wife while vacationing aboard a cruise ship, caused John to smile but, hope the recounting was more fiction than reality. In his present condition however, fiction and fact were impossible concepts for John to comprehend. Still, the venerable gentleman could weave a yarn.

Another caller appeared in the form of a tall, gangly young man speaking a near-incomprehensible language. Young Ichabod Crane, as John quickly dubbed him, seemed to take great pride in discussing the enormous pool of technical knowledge available which, with some creativity, could be applied to the practical use of music in creative dance. John didn't understand most of the theories but, the idea of fusing science and art, employing computer wizardry, seemed fascinating. If this young man were an apparition, John thought him to be a very clever one.

A sedated Mr. Coyle was not too desensitized to recognize a true hallucination when one materialized. At least, he held the premise to be true. Why else would an ageing movie star seem so genuinely interested in an acting career which John had never pursued? She was a very charming and erudite delusion however, and John enjoyed her psychogenic stimulation immensely.

"The Freakin' Man" came very close to lassoing John and pulling him back across the bridge to reality. As the bouncer listened to his diminutive guest complain about how his "business obligations" had robbed him of his "freakin' youth" and, how his life was in dire need of some "freakin' good luck for once", John knew that he was somehow inextricably connected to this pessimistic man/vision. *How* they were bound together however, eluded the big man.

Sweet Molly

On the eighth day of his hospitalization, John Coyle awoke and knew exactly where he was and how he had arrived there.

He also knew who the beautiful lady was sitting at his bedside. It was Molly. Although she looked concerned, her smile reflected her great relief to see John in his present state of awareness.

John's entire body ached and, his face seemed tight and unresponsive to movement but, he was the first to speak. "It's good to see you, Molly. Thank you for being here." John's voice was weak and raspy.

"You're welcome, John. It's good to see you too. There were times when…" Molly cast her eyes downward. She sat in silence.

John continued. "Everyone was here, weren't they, Molly? I just couldn't seem to focus too well on the conversation at times. Must have been some heavy stuff I was being served at this resort. I'm only used to beer." John attempted to coax a smile to Molly's face. It worked.

"I think you're going to be just fine, John." Molly reached over and took the bouncer's hand. She was pleased that the worst was over. "Yes, everyone was here for you, John. That's what people do when they care about someone. Besides, The Sunset just isn't the same without you underfoot."

John smiled, with effort, and squeezed Molly's hand.

"This isn't the first time here, is it, Molly?"

"This is the eighth day, John."

"And you were here every day?"

"Yeah, I'm not a big fan of daytime television. The coffee's good here too."

John slowly shook his head. Suddenly, time seemed of paramount importance. Life was short. "I've gotta get out of here, Molly. There are things I have to do." The bouncer needed to ask the question that was pressing on his consciousness. "Where's Scarlet, Molly? Is she okay?"

"You're not going anywhere for a while, John." Molly's voice seemed to take on a slight chill. "You've been through hell but, you just don't know it yet. I'm sure that Scarlet is fine but, I'm not the one to ask. Your friend, Mr. Spinelli is far more knowledgeable than I. I got to know him a little over the last week. He's quite the character but, he cares for you like a father, John. He'll fill you in soon. Right now, you should rest. We need you back at the club but, we need you back healthy. Okay?"

John wanted to press on with his inquiries but decided to yield to Molly's advice. He was tired. He had also seen Molly wield a cleaver. In his present state, he opted for prudence. "Okay, Molly. You're right. I just want to thank you again for coming. I really appreciate it. Please thank everyone back at the club and tell them I'll see them soon."

"Alright, John, I will. Just concentrate on getting better." Molly rose, smiled and, departed.

Suddenly, John Coyle felt drained. He wanted to drift back to a healing state of somnolence and dream of Scarlet. Instead, Molly's face was the last image he visualized as sleep overtook him.

Even Bouncers
Require Sustenance

John Coyle slept for fifteen straight hours. When he awoke, he felt refreshed and very hungry. It had been awhile since he had consumed anything vaguely resembling a "Mucho Burger". Yesterday's soup and Jello, served by a motherly, cherubic lady, after Molly had left, had only teased John's palate. Today, he was famished.

Within minutes of propping himself up in bed, John's prayers were answered by the same cheerful attendant who had served him the delectable repast the day before. As she approached his side, John discerned her name tag. The kindly genie's name was Joan.

"Good afternoon, Mr. Coyle. How are we today?"

"I'm fine, Joan, and, how are you?"

"I'm here to serve you with a smile, Mr. Coyle. Some good news too! The doctor said that today you could have whatever you wanted. You're a big man, Mr. Coyle. You must be famished!"

"Joan, you really are an angel! Please though, my name is John."

Joan seemed pleased to be entrusted with the familiarity. "Well then, John, what would you like for dinner?"

John thought for a very brief moment. "Joan, I'd like the biggest, thickest, juiciest steak you can possibly find! Medium done, please. I'd also love a huge mound of fries with mushroom gravy served on a separate platter, if possible. Maybe a Caesar salad would be good too. I love the croutons when they get a bit soggy. Oh, and, Joan, could I have a large, frosty mug of beer, please? Domestic is fine. That would be great! Thanks, Joan."

The big man's new confidante chuckled at his request but, with a straight face, and, the lofty tone of a snooty head waiter, replied: "I shall do my best, sir. I only hope that this simple establishment can fulfil such refined gastronomic needs." Joan inclined her head slightly and disappeared.

John could only hope.

Joan returned in twenty-eight minutes. After adjusting John's bedside table and pillows, she withdrew his meal from her stainless steel cart and presented the feast to its ravenous recipient.

The fare was not quite what John had hoped for but, he was certainly not going to return it to the chef. Two small scoops of mashed potatoes, topped with two equally minute dollops of congealed, unrecognizable goo had replaced the mountain of fries smothered in mushroom gravy that Mr. Coyle had conceived in his doldrums of hunger. A child-sized plastic glass of apple juice had supplanted the chilled mug of beer. A soggy lettuce salad was substituted for the Caesar. There was steak though. The Salisbury looked rubbery but, edible. So did the Jello.

It was simply the best meal that John Coyle had ever envisioned!

"Thank you, Joan. This looks wonderful!"

"You're welcome, John. I know it's not quite what you were hoping for but, it's the best we could do. Oh, and here's something else you might enjoy." From the bottom rack of the cart, Joan withdrew several dog-eared issues of The National Geographic and presented them to her incapacitated ward. "Some of them aren't even that old."

John smiled and accepted the gifts with gratitude. "I really appreciate your kindness, Joan. I'm getting spoiled. All I'm gonna do is eat, read a bit and, get more sleep. Sort of like being on vacation!"

The matronly attendant laughed. "Sounds like a good idea to me! Get plenty of rest because tomorrow may be a busy day. Someone will pick up the dishes later. Have a good night, Mr. Coyle."

"You too, Joan. It's John though."

"Okay, John." The benign support giver smiled and exited.

Scarlet's Fate

At seven thirty, the next morning, John was awakened by a nurse he didn't recognize. She was very young and very pretty. The patient felt much older. He wished he had shaved earlier. The stitches made the simple process quite difficult.

"Good morning, Mr. Coyle. I'm sorry to wake you but, the doctor will be in shortly to see you."

"That's okay, miss. I'm glad you did. It's about time I got myself into gear. I'm usually a lot more active."

"Oh, I can see that, Mr. Coyle." The young nurse smiled.

John smiled back. He tried to expand his chest. His ribs hurt.

"I'll let you alone now, Mr. Coyle. Just ring if you need anything. Anything at all." The pretty coquette smiled impishly, pivoted vivaciously and, left the room.

The bouncer rose from his bed deftly and with haste. He needed to shave.

About an hour later, Mr. John Coyle was joined by Dr. Nigel Hyde-Edwards, a middle-aged, bespectacled gentleman who spoke in a thick, cultured British accent.

Morning salutations were exchanged.

Dr. Hyde-Edwards began his examination.

Several minutes later, the physician concluded his deliberative inspection. He seemed very pleased. "Well, young man, you certainly seem to possess remarkable recuperative powers. I think we can remove your sutures tomorrow or the next day. Your ribs are going to be tender for a while though and you might want to favour your weakened shoulder. Nothing too physical. We're going to keep you here for a few days longer until you regain some strength. I'll check in on you tomorrow. Any questions, Mr. Coyle?"

"No, doctor but, I just want to thank you and everyone else though for taking such good care of me. I owe you a lot."

"You're entirely welcome, young man. I'm pleased that we could help."

John Coyle extended his hand and the two men shook in silence.

Two hours after Joan had recovered John's lunch dishes, the bouncer was paid another visit. At first, the big man hadn't noticed the arrival of his guest. He was staring out the window thinking of Scarlet. A single word broke the spell.

"John."

John turned toward the source of the voice. He knew that it was Mr. Spinelli.

Without speaking, the two men took a few steps toward each other and embraced for several seconds. Words weren't necessary.

Finally, John tenderly withdrew from his old friend. "Thanks for coming, Mr. Spinelli. Molly tells me this isn't the first time. I can't tell you how much this means…" The bouncer found the appropriate words difficult to articulate.

"Of course I come, John! What else can I do with checkers partner…temporarily incapacitated?"

Both men grinned.

John took a deep breath.

Mr. Spinelli knew what was forthcoming.

"Mr. Spinelli, I want to know all the details of that day, including what happened to Scarlet. Don't leave anything out. I have the right to know. Please tell me."

"We sit."

Both men sat. John on the bedside, Mr. Spinelli on a rigid hospital chair.

"Okay, John. You do have the right to know. Scarlet also wanna you told the truth." Mr. Spinelli paused briefly, then resumed. "When Scarlet realize…severity of situation, she drive to my house with great haste. She inna hysterical state. She tella me what happened. We phone for emergency assistance, then drive back. I drive. I also bring my baseball bat. When we get to parking lot, nobody there, jus' you. You very bad. Ambulance come an' you taken to hospital. We follow.

"We remain at hospital many hours. We talk. We worry. Finally, very nice doctor talk to us. He say that you will be fine but needa mucha rest. He say we should go. Nothing we can do. We go.

"We drive back to my place. Scarlet not wanna go back to club. It is late but, we talk an' drink wine. Many truths revealed. Mucha understanding…attained in reciprocal fashion. We talk until dawn. I fall asleep inna my chair. I wake up around two o'clock. Scarlet is gone. I knew she would be.

"I drive to your place of employment. Mr. Kmetzko tella me that Scarlet and he discuss things. Scarlet say she musta go. Mr. Kmetzko understand. There were no bad feelings. Scarlet leave."

"Where did she go, Mr. Spinelli?" John's voice was urgent.

"I do not know, John. Maybe it does not matter."

"Why did she go?" John demanded an answer.

"John, inna opinion of this old man, Scarlet leave because she care about you more than she care about herself. She wanna you to have the life that will not be haunted by ghosts from her past. She wanna you to make new start… to be shed of…burdens."

"But, I love her, Mr. Spinelli!"

"Maybe you do, John. Maybe loving her and being in love not the same thing. Maybe she love you too. Please, try to understand, my friend."

John buried his face in his hands. There was nothing he could say.

Mr. Spinelli rose and slowly made his way to the door. Before leaving, he stopped and turned.

"You are very fortunate individual, John Coyle. Not many men have so many people who really care about them. Think about this. I see you soon."

Mr. Spinelli quietly took his leave.

Mr. Coyle thought about his friend's words until sleep finally overtook him.

Threadbare but, Bouncing Back

At eleven thirty-seven on Thursday morning, Dr. Nigel Hyde-Edwards paid a visit to Mr. Coyle's bedside.

"Good morning, Mr. Coyle. How are you feeling today? Time to get rid of the sutures, I believe."

"I'm fine, thank you, doctor. How are you, sir?"

"Very well, thank you. We can do this right here if you like. Kindly prop yourself up a bit though and, I'll have a look. Slide your gown down a bit so that I can examine your chest wounds, please."

John Coyle did what he was asked.

After a thorough examination, Dr. Hyde-Edwards was ready to proceed. "Some physicians allow a competent nurse to remove sutures but, personally, I prefer to finish what I started. Ready, Mr. Coyle?"

"Whenever you're ready, doctor. Thank you for your personal attention."

Dr. Hyde-Edwards smiled and nodded. "Alright then. Let's begin, sir."

The task took much longer than John had anticipated. His surgeon was as meticulous in removing the sutures as he had been in placing them. There were a few times when John felt a twinge of discomfort but, not many. A minor inconvenience.

Finally, Dr. Hyde-Edwards completed his painstaking labour. He seemed pleased.

"Well, Mr. Coyle, I hope that wasn't too bad. You look quite good if I do say so myself!"

"Thanks again, doctor for everything. Your dedication is certainly appreciated."

"My pleasure, young man. You're a good patient."

John decided to press on. "Doctor, I was wondering when I could go home."

"I can dismiss you on Sunday, if you promise to stay home for another week or so. I don't want you doing anything but resting. Once back at work, you're to do nothing strenuous until you're able. I know what your job entails, Mr. Coyle and, I also know that you are an intelligent man. Do we have an understanding, sir?"

"We do, doctor."

The two men shook hands.

Welcome Visits

For the next three days, John Coyle's life settled into comfortable routine. The bouncer was biding his time while making the best of his constrained situation.

John took great pride in devising new means of persuading Joan, his considerate attendant to deliver meals which were completely out of the realm of possibility. Mealtimes, although repetitive, became a bit more of a diversion due to shared badinage. Occasionally, Joan would actually succeed in smuggling an extra Salisbury steak to her esteemed patient.

Visits from old friends helped pass the time and seemed to boost John's morale when too much thinking about Scarlet put him in a temporary morose frame of mind.

Charlie and Delbert always brought sparkle to John's drab environment.

The bouncer was enthralled with Charlie's tale of how Mike Murphy and several members of The Lonesome

Desperados motorcycle gang had filled in for him on a regular basis throughout his convalescence. Amazing!

Delbert's enthusiasm for future projects and novel technical innovations made John marvel at his young friend's inventiveness. Delbert's unique verbal delivery often rendered his most serious scholarly dissertations almost ludicrous though. To the bouncer, Delbert's lectures seemed comparable to Daffy Duck expounding upon a neoteric concept developed by Stephen Hawking.

Still, several of Delbert's ideas, although somewhat radical, seemed quite plausible to the bouncer. One concept, involving light and colour sensing cells seemed especially intriguing. According to Delbert, if the present neon sign stretching over the double doors of The Sunset Club's façade could be rigged to "read" the light values and colours of the actual outside conditions and, interpret these signals by illuminating only the appropriate array of tinted cells, the sign would now be in sync with the reality of not only sunsets but, beautiful starry nights. During cloudy or grey conditions, the sign could be switched to manual. The club's name, for the most part, would reflect actuality. Its interior would bend the concept per tradition.

If nothing else, thought John, *Delbert is one funky and far-out dude.*

Usually, at around one o'clock, Mr. Spinelli would visit, a checkers game always in hand. Mr. Spinelli would consistently win. No mercy was shown to his incapacitated friend. If John wanted to talk about Scarlet, Mr. Spinelli would listen with understanding and compassion. The elderly gentleman would offer an opinion or personal insight only if he were asked. Instinctively, he knew that it did his young friend a world of good to simply vent his thoughts and feelings.

Molly would also call on a daily basis, just before reporting to work. Nothing too serious was broached.

Daily events at The Sunset, the eccentricities of their fellow co-workers and, the current state of John's health were innocuous topics both were comfortable in discussing. Keep things light.

Still, when the time came for Molly to depart, John felt a strange sense of regret. The emotion was, in a melancholy fashion, coupled with guilt. The bouncer felt reprehensible for visualizing Molly's next visit with such anticipation. He was self-reproachful for harbouring such a feeling but, found it impossible to dispel. The thought persisted.

Discharged!

Late Sunday afternoon, after a mandatory examination by Dr. Hyde-Edwards, John Coyle was discharged from the hospital.

His gratitude and thanks were bestowed upon Joan and, an invitation for dinner in the near future, was accepted by the blushing, warm-hearted attendant. John knew what he would order…Salisbury steak and Jello. Tradition should be respected.

Since hospital protocol must at all times be obeyed, John reluctantly allowed himself to be wheeled out the front door of the hospital by the same young, pretty nurse with whom he had cajoled several days earlier. Today, the bouncer had shaved. Today, he had assured the very attractive nurse that he would have no difficulty in carrying his one suitcase in his lap while she pushed. The nurse's response was quite gratifying to the bouncer: "With those muscles, it looks like you could carry ten suitcases with no problem!" John's chest expanded. It didn't hurt.

In the emergency parking area, John could see Mr. Spinelli approaching. He signalled his companion to break. The bouncer climbed out of the chair, transferred his suitcase to his left hand, raised himself to his full height and, extended his right hand to the nurse. They shook. John's grip was firm. The pretty caregiver smiled coyly.

By this time, Mr. Spinelli had joined the pair. His smile was less provocative. "Hi, John! I no wanna break up the moment but…"

"That's okay, my friend. We were just saying goodbye."

Mr. Spinelli's smile grew broader.

The nurse set off, pushing her wheelchair toward the hospital. She stopped, turned around and, winked.

John felt very healthy.

Mr. Spinelli led John to the old Chevy. John threw his suitcase onto the back seat.

Mr. Spinelli insisted on driving.

The drive home took very little time.

Home Sweet Home

Once John's single suitcase had been unceremoniously dropped upon his bed, the newly discharged freeman checked the contents of his trailer's refrigerator, poked his head out of the door and, offered a proposition to his venerable friend seated at the table on the deck. "Mr. Spinelli, I have four beers and a bottle of red wine just waiting to be opened. Would you care to join me in downing these cold thirst quenchers?"

"I would be most delighted to…assist in dispensing with these…earthly libations! I no wanna see you drink too mucha on first day home."

"Thank you, old friend. Care for some cold pizza?"

After nearly two hours of catching up on petty gossip in the trailer park, as well as solving every major problem existing in the universe, John Coyle and his long-time companion realized that they had depleted their meagre supply of alcohol. It was only eight thirty!

"No worry, my friend! Givva me a few minutes an' I... remedy this situation!"

Mr. Spinelli was a gentleman who was always true to his word. He quickly departed to his own trailer and, in a few moments, returned, carrying a large bottle of red wine in each bony hand.

"I hope vintage is acceptable, my friend!"

"You're a lifesaver, Mr. Spinelli, a real lifesaver!"

Mr. Spinelli smiled proudly.

Two hours passed. By now, the entire galaxy was a safer and much better place.

As John bade Mr. Spinelli a good night, he reluctantly sought council from his sagacious confidant. "Mr. Spinelli, I was thinking of giving Molly a call just before she started work tomorrow. What do you think?"

"I think that would be an excellent idea, John."

That night, the bouncer slept like a baby.

Time Spent at Home

Perhaps, as a result of a single phone call, the following week passed most pleasantly.

There were the customary games of skill with Mr. Spinelli which John always enjoyed losing. Besides, drinking wine and beer under the stars with the winner, always helped to assuage the bouncer's slightly damaged ego.

Visits by Charlie and Delbert were brief but, always kinetic and most entertaining. Both uncle and nephew seemed incapable of oral repose.

Charlie's verbosity consisted primarily of "getting out of the freakin' business" and, warming his "tired bones" in Florida.

Delbert, on the other hand, seemed to flourish in his present environment. Up-to-date systematic innovations as applied to the enhancement of The Sunset Club, seemed to permeate his every thought. The younger Kmetzko appeared convinced that it was his sole purpose in life to convert everyone else to his religion of technology.

Throughout his telephone conversation with Molly on Monday evening, John had tried to remain casual and unassuming. He thanked the young lady for her visits while he was hospitalized. He discussed various aspects of their respective workloads at The Sunset. He confided in Molly about how much he valued the friendship of Mr. Spinelli and the Kmetzkos. The bouncer also managed, in what he thought were clever and surreptitious interjections, to give Molly his phone number and specific directions to his trailer. John assured the pretty cook that if she ever needed him for any reason, she would know how to locate him. Molly felt flattered the first couple of times that John offered her this private enlightenment. After three or four further proclamations, the information became *slightly* repetitive. Finally, with a laugh she could no longer suppress, Molly cut the conversation short. "John, would you like me to pop by for a bit before work tomorrow?"

"That would be great, Molly! Are you sure you know how to get here?"

Women and Workouts

By Wednesday morning, John Coyle felt physically invigorated and, emotionally stronger. Molly's visit the night before proved more potent than any elixir he had ever received from hospital staff.

He still thought of Scarlet with love and compassion, with great frequency, throughout every hour of wakefulness. What was somewhat perplexing to John however, was the fact that it was Molly who occupied his thoughts just before drifting off to sleep the night before. He hoped she would visit again tonight though.

As the bouncer set off at a leisurely pace toward the trailer park gym, it was not the thought of beautiful women that filled his mind. He was envisaging the workout ahead. It had been many days since he had demanded anything arduous of his body. The workout today would have to be light. Focus upon the entire body. Avoid numerous sets. Be smart.

At the end of the hour, John felt exhausted yet pleased. Experience had prevailed. He had reined himself in when he thought he could do more. There was no sense in risking an injury. It wouldn't take long before he was handling the heavy poundage. Maybe tomorrow, he could focus upon one or two body parts. Maybe add a little more resistance. The ribs felt fine. There was nothing he could do about the scars.

At about seven, John noticed Molly approaching his deck. He was seated upon one of his comfortable, old canvas chairs. He was thinking of partaking in a beer. He arose to greet his guest. "Hi, Molly. Did the taxi drop you off at The Sunset?"

"Yes. It's just a few minutes' walk here and, it gives me time to think about what I have to do tonight. By the way, everyone at work said they missed you. They said that it's just not the same without you. Everybody's chipping in but, they're not pros."

"Well, tell them I'll be back soon. I miss not having a job. Retirement's not for me." John was pleased that Molly thought of him as a professional.

"How are you feeling, John? Getting your strength back?" Molly's voice emitted true concern.

"Well, actually I had a pretty fair workout today. I didn't set any gym records but, I don't think it'll take too long to get back into it."

"Charlie will be glad to hear that, John! Mike Murphy and those motorcycle guys are doing their best but, they just don't have your flair."

Again, John was pleased that the young lady held him in such esteem.

"Thanks, Molly. It's still good of them to fill in. I'm planning on starting in on Monday night, if it's okay with Charlie. I'm sure he'll be around sometime this week. I'll check with him then."

"You won't be met with any opposition, John. You might even get a hug!"

John smiled at the mental image. He smiled a lot during the next hour. So did Molly.

Maybe some kinds of scars would eventually fade. Maybe the bouncer just needed time.

Soothing Ritual

For the next few days, John Coyle found himself blanketed in comfortable routine. There were the checkers games and customary spirit samplings with Mr. Spinelli, enlightening bouts of information dispatching by cohorts from The Sunset, the daily workouts from which John grew increasingly trenchant and, the nightly visits from Molly, prior to beginning her shift.

It was the time spent with Molly that the bouncer cherished most. Together, the peaceful enforcer and the very pretty short order cook discussed everything and nothing at the same time. John's deck had become a minute island of respite from worldly concerns. Nothing too serious was discussed and recent events of gravity were never broached. It was an unspoken understanding which both respected. For John, the manner in which Molly spoke carried as much substance as her delivery. He enjoyed watching her and took great pleasure in observing her every expression and nuance. The corner of the right side of her mouth turned up slightly higher than the left when Molly smiled. Molly would often uplift her face when she laughed. Molly's pale blue eyes seemed to capture the sun's rays. Molly, Molly, Molly. Still, the bouncer never made the mistake of filtering out the lady's words for the sake of basking in her visual subtleties. He remembered Molly's skills with the cleaver with great clarity.

Often at night however, before sleep overcame him, John Coyle's mind would pulsate more forcefully than his satiated muscles. His thoughts would jump from the present to troubled events of the recent past. Images of Scarlet would flood the big man's thoughts. Flashbacks of pain. Unanswered questions robbed him of peace. John Coyle had found no closure.

First Night Back

John Coyle stood before the massive steel doors of The Sunset Club at precisely eight thirty, Monday night. It had been several weeks since he had found himself in this situation. The bouncer felt apprehensive. He hoped that he remembered all the card tricks. He took a deep breath and pushed open the portal.

The few paces through the dark hallway leading to the turnstile seemed to take an eternity to cover. Tentatively, John Coyle touched the heavy post from which the arms of the stile radiated. He turned to his right.

"Oh, John...I..." Wanda Goldman was unable to continue her thought. Instantaneously, she emerged through the small door leading into and out of the ticket booth and stood in the passageway gazing up at her friend. "John, I'm so sorry. I don't know what to say." Mrs. Goldman's voice quivered and tears streamed from her eyes.

John opened his arms and the warm-hearted ticket taker fell against his chest. Her sobs wracked her entire being.

"Now, now, Ms. Taylor, there will be other auditions from which I shall emerge with more success! This nonfulfillment of employment is temporary, I'm sure! In no time at all, the perfect script will arrive on the gentle winds of fortune!"

Mrs. Goldman picked up her cue. "I'm sure you're right, Mr. Barrymore. It's just that the hearts of artists like ourselves can sometimes swell with empathy, thus causing an emotional deluge. Please, sir, forgive me for addressing you in such familiar terms." Mrs. Goldman had regained most of her composure. She was glad to be in character.

"Please, think nothing of it, Ms. Taylor. May I ask you a rather intimate question, madam?"

"Of course, sir."

"When we find ourselves away from the admiring eyes of the demanding public, may I, on occasion, call you, Elizabeth?"

"It would be an honour, Mr. Barrymore."

"Thank you, Elizabeth."

"Please pass, John."

The bouncer felt that he might be able to deal the cards after all.

Stepping into the vast entertainment room of The Sunset, John Coyle was completely taken aback at the sight of his employer, co-workers and, several friends lined up in front of the long mahogany bar as if waiting to pass muster. They had been anticipating the triumphant return of their sergeant-at-arms.

As John approached the troops, he noticed that each member of the file displayed a wide grin proudly exhibited on his open, familiar face. Each had passed inspection with flying colours!

"How're you doin', John? Glad you're back! Ready to get to work?" Charlie was the first to speak.

John responded. "I'm ready, boss. Good to be back."

More greetings, handshakes and, light hearted banter ensued.

Gradually, everyone departed to assume personal responsibilities.

As Molly set off for the kitchen, she turned and winked at John. He winked back. She was wearing her short, black miniskirt. Her legs were very long.

John smiled, turned and, began scanning the room for his initial vantage point. It was good to be back.

That night, the magic was good.

To Every Time

For the next two weeks, John Coyle was kept busy on the job and during his off hours.

Since the inception of their affiliation, Charlie Kmetzko and Mike Murphy had developed a relationship which was based on admiration tinged with avarice. Most of their money-making schemes tended to centre on the concept of marketing meat. After only a few days of resuming his chosen calling, John was asked to assist in one such venture. Charlie and Mike Murphy had purchased a used candy dispensing machine and had stocked it with several varieties of beef jerky. For the paltry sum of one dollar, customers could now enjoy a carnal taste sensation wrapped in cellophane. It took the bouncer almost an hour, with the help of a sturdy dolly, to position the weighty device to a location which satisfied both entrepreneurs. John hoped the idea would fly.

Delbert's fertile imagination had continued to flourish in John's absence. "Dig it, big guy. All you have to do is mount these screens to the ceiling above the stage. I'll be able to push a button and project anything from sunny skies to starry constellations up there! Even Mars, man! Far-out, huh? Our own planetarium, amigo!" John arrived four hours early the next day in order to comply with the disc jockey's request. It worked splendidly during testing.

The company of Mr. Spinelli was always treasured. Simple games of skill and wine tasting under clear skies were diversions that John Coyle appreciated. Mr. Spinelli's tales of love and intrigue were gems to be savoured. "John, I ever tella you 'bout younga girl name, Flossie? Her sudden demise at such a tender age was…both shocking and tragic."

Numerous and arduous hours at the gym had begun to produce results. The bouncer's body had begun to respond. He had gained strength with each successive session. His weight had increased to within five pounds of the customary two-hundred, seventeen pounds that he liked to carry. John felt good. He felt strong.

Throughout the duration of his initial return to The Sunset Club, the intervals which he spent with Molly were the moments which caused John Coyle great anxiety and tremendous tranquility at the same time. On each occasion in which he found himself alone with the statuesque beauty, he felt like a kid, out on his first date. Butterflies fluttered in his stomach. His palms grew sweaty. He was sure that he was developing a stutter. Within a few heartbeats however, John's condition always changed dramatically. He felt comfortable and relaxed. He could say anything. Molly would listen. She would soothe him. Molly could lessen pain. Molly could fade scars.

Still, there were nights when the big man couldn't sleep.

Auld Lang Syne

At ten o'clock on the Monday evening marking John Coyle's third week back on the job, the bouncer decided that it was time to shift positions. Q.P. Doll had just completed her debut performance at The Sunset. Judging by the applause, the audience found her to be a prize. From his post near the exit on the west wall, John slowly wound his way around the vacant stage toward the bar. It would be good to touch base with Charlie.

As he neared to within thirty feet of his employer's working area, The Sunset's mediator froze in his tracks. There, at the bar, casually sipping beer, sat Tweedledee and Tweedledum with their keeper, Mr. Lank-and-Greasy.

Over the years, because of necessity, John Coyle had learned to make fast decisions. He now drew upon experience. Turning slowly around, so as not to be noticed by the malignant trio, the bouncer retraced his steps until he once again found himself hidden behind the runway. He leaned against the north wall near the exit. His breathing seemed strained. His face grew pallid. His fists clenched. The bouncer had always preferred diplomacy but, he now realized that he had no control over his present status. He had become Mr. Hyde. His adrenal transformation was complete. John Coyle was not proud of his metamorphosis but, he was resolute. He felt a strange sense of surrealism overtake him. He had a job to do.

The next dancer would take the stage in a couple of minutes. There was time. John, while making his previous rounds, had noticed four members of The Lonesome Desperados motorcycle gang chugging beer in a booth along the west side of The Playroom. He had smiled and nodded at them. They had returned the gestures. The bikers had often covered for John while he was convalescing. They had worked for beer. They had caused no trouble then and, they were causing no trouble now.

John Coyle took a seat next to one of the bikers and began a conversation in hushed, conspiratorial tones. By the time the second dancer's routine had ended, a deal had been struck. The bouncer and the bikers rose. They shook hands. Three bikers set off toward the three exits. The remaining Desperado made his way to the entrance of the room. The four gang members were under contract. The bouncer had given orders. No one would be able to flee The Playroom.

Charlie Kmetzko raised his hand and smiled as John Coyle quickly approached the bar. Charlie Kmetzko promptly lowered his hand. A solemn look of concern replaced his grin. For as long as he had known John, The Sunset's employer had never seen such an expression of sheer venomous loathing frozen on his friend's face. The bartender had never seen his employee brandish an empty beer bottle by the neck in club-like fashion.

John drew within three feet of the bar.

"Okay, John, I can see there's trouble. I'll make the call." Charlie's voice quaked.

"No, Charlie. Don't touch the phone. The trouble hasn't even started." John's voice was calm and resolute. Charlie wisely obeyed the command.

The three depraved gorillas turned on their stools to face John. The tall slimy leader spoke first. "Well, if it ain't Sir Galahad himself! Hope you're not thinkin' of stopping us from checkin' out the new talent. Gotta make a living, you know." The tall man sneered.

John stared at the greaseball. A faint smile played across the bouncer's mouth. "Yeah, I'm gonna stop you." John swung the glass bludgeon with the force of a catapult. The blow landed squarely on the left temple of the slab of flesh seated in closest proximity to John Coyle's batting arm. The monster crashed to the floor. He didn't get up. The second mountain rose from his stool. The bouncer had counted on that. A swiftly placed knee to the groin dropped the beast to all fours. A barstool smashed across his back rendered the animal motionless.

"Okay, okay, I get the point! I'm leavin'. You win. I don't want no more trouble." Slick was trembling.

"You're not going anywhere, punk. Take a look around. There's no way out."

The tall man scanned the room. All exits were blocked by very big, very hairy, very mean looking guards. He swung around to face the bouncer. As he did, the weasel quickly withdrew a stiletto from his pocket, snapped it open and, pointed it at John. The knife shook in his hand.

"Not this time, dirtbag." The bouncer feinted with his right fist. His adversary followed the movement with his stiletto. John blasted a bone-crushing left jab to the tall man's mouth. Blood splattered. Broken teeth were spat out. The lanky coward reeled in pain. John grabbed the knife with his right hand and threw his opponent against the bar with his left. The bouncer pressed the tip of the switchblade into the neck of the terrified bully. A drop of blood appeared.

"Stop, John! You're better than that! Please, John, listen to me! It's over!" Molly was crying.

John Coyle turned toward the pleading voice. As he gazed at Molly for what seemed an eternity, a demon within him seemed to take wing. The big man sighed. He pushed his beaten foe onto a bar stool. "Don't move." The bloodied man was quick to obey.

"You want me to make that call now, John? Let's get this freakin' trash outa here!" Charlie sensed that his friend had returned.

"Good idea, boss. Here, take this blade too. Cops might like a souvenir." John smiled. It was his old smile.

Just a Minor Inconvenience

In less than an hour, The Sunset was functioning as if nothing had ever interrupted the magic show. Delbert was pressing hidden buttons. Charlie was complaining. Dancers were breaking in new routines. Customers were enjoying cold beer. The bouncer was keeping the peace.

At around twelve, during a short break, John found himself seated at the bar discussing real estate prices in Florida with Charlie. As Molly emerged from the kitchen however, he abruptly excused himself and rose from his stool. Charlie understood.

John caught up with the cook.

"Molly, do you think I could drive you home tonight? I know that Charlie wouldn't mind if I left early, especially tonight."

"I'd like that very much, John. Long, crazy night." Molly's eyes were very blue.

"Yeah, crazy night. Once in a while, Molly. I'm glad it's over. You okay?"

Molly took John's hand.

John Patrick Coyle felt unbeatable. He was the bouncer.

"Molly?"

"Yes, John."

"Do you like Salisbury steak and Jello?"

Molly laughed. The right corner of her mouth turned up slightly.